Closely Observed
Theatre

JONATHAN CROALL edited the magazine *StageWrite* for the National Theatre for fifteen years, and subsequently edited the programmes at the Old Vic. Formerly an editor in publishing, now a biographer and theatre historian, he is the author of over twenty books, notably the acclaimed biographies *John Gielgud: Matinee Idol to Movie Star* and *Sybil Thorndike: A Star of Life*.

His other books include *The Coming of Godot: A Short History of a Masterpiece*, which was shortlisted for the 2005 Theatre Book Prize; the collection *Buzz Buzz! Playwrights, Actors and Directors at the National Theatre*; three books in the series The National Theatre at Work – *Hamlet Observed*, *Peter Hall's 'Bacchai'*, and *Inside the Molly House*; *The Wit and Wisdom (and Gaffes) of John Gielgud* and *In Search of Gielgud: A Biographer's Tale*.

His book *Forgotten Stars: My Father and the British Silent Film World* is also published by Fantom.

Closely Observed Theatre

From the National to the Old Vic

Jonathan Croall

First published in 2014 by Fantom Films
fantomfilms.co.uk

A catalogue record for this book is available from the British Library.

Paperback edition ISBN: 978-1-78196-117-9

Typeset by Phil Reynolds Media Services, Leamington Spa
Printed and bound in the UK by ImprintDigital.com

Contents

Introduction

WHEN IT COMES TO THEATRE, London is acknowledged to be one of the most exciting cities in the world. Over the last twenty years I have been lucky enough to work as a kind of journalist-in-residence in two of its greatest theatres, the National and the Old Vic, watching rehearsals, interviewing leading actors and directors, and reporting on many plays, projects and ideas.

During my time at the National I wrote books about productions of *Hamlet*, *Mother Clap's Molly House* and *Bacchai*, observing their directors John Caird, Nicholas Hytner and Peter Hall in action. While editing the theatre's magazine *StageWrite* I also wrote articles on a range of productions, projects and playwrights on the South Bank. I then spent the next five years as the editor of the Old Vic programmes, most of which included a feature of mine based on the rare opportunity I was given to sit in on rehearsals. This book brings together some fifty of the pieces that I wrote, which highlight the impressive variety of work taking place in those two theatres.

My connection with the Old Vic covered several years of Kevin Spacey's artistic directorship, which gave me the opportunity to see the ferociously talented Hollywood star at work close up. But this was not just a matter of observing his consummate skill as an actor. In addition to observing how he went about developing his characters in plays such as *A Moon for the Misbegotten* and *The Philadelphia Story*, I watched him in action as a director on the American play *Complicit*, and talked to him about the opening play in his regime, *Cloaca*, which he also directed. I was lucky enough to observe the techniques of two other American directors: the legendary Robert Altman, brought over near the end of his long film career to direct Arthur Miller's *Resurrection Blues*; and Jerry Zaks, the winner of several Tony Awards for his productions on Broadway, who directed *The Philadelphia Story*.

At the Vic I also had the chance to watch some of the leading British directors in rehearsal. They included Peter Hall, working meticulously on Shaw's *Pygmalion*; Howard Davies, helping his actors to tease out their characters' inner life in O'Neill's *A Moon for the Misbegotten*; Sean Holmes, emphasising the political nature and modern relevance of Osborne's *The Entertainer*; Ed Hall, working with his all-male company Propeller on meaning and motivation in *Twelfth Night*; and Sean Mathias, keeping the pantomime spirit alive for a revival of *Aladdin*.

Along the way I had a rare bird's-eye view of the very different approaches of many star actors to creating their parts: David Suchet and Richard Dreyfuss in *Complicit*, Eve Best in *A Moon for the Misbegotten*, Tim Pigott-Smith and Michelle Dockery in *Pygmalion*, Lesley Manville and Diana Rigg in *All About My Mother*, Jennifer Ehle and Julia

Mackenzie in *The Philadelphia Story*, James Fox and Maximilian Schell in *Resurrection Blues*, and many more.

Howard Davies, Kevin Spacey and Eve Best shared with me their thoughts about working on *A Moon for the Misbegotten*, while Matthew Warchus joined with Kevin Spacey, Jeff Goldblum and Laura Michelle Kelly to talk about interpreting Mamet's *Speed-the-Plow*. I also heard from Ian McKellen, Roger Allam and Maureen Lipman about the joys of playing in pantomime; from Trevor Nunn about his approach to directing *Richard II*, and its resonance today; from Peter Gill, Rosamund Pike, Kenneth Cranham and Andrew Woodall about working on Patrick Hamilton's *Gaslight*; and from Hugh Bonneville and the rest of the *Cloaca* company about their various characters in Maria Goos' play.

Over at the National there was an absorbing variety of work to cover. There were more sessions observing rehearsals, notably those for children's theatre productions: they included watching Alan Ayckbourn direct his own *Mr A's Amazing Maze Plays*, and Ultz putting together the children's show *Dragon*. There were different approaches to Shakespeare to report on: a workshop for students on *Henry V*, a production for schools of *The Tempest*. Musicals also featured strongly: I talked to choreographer Matthew Bourne about his key role in the production of *My Fair Lady*, and wrote a lengthy piece showing how the various National departments were involved in putting together their hit production of Sondheim's *A Little Night Music*.

I looked at the work going on in the Studio, the National's laboratory for research and experiment, and at innovative schemes such as the Transformation project, which created a new space in the Lyttelton. I also recorded discussions with Marianne Elliott, Katie Mitchell and Melly

Still about women directors; heard from Tom Morris about the National's plans to link up with several experimental theatre groups; and reported on the views of Simon Russell Beale and other actors involved in Trevor Nunn and John Caird's NT ensemble company. Diana Rigg and Denis Quilley talked to me about the National's move from the Old Vic to the South Bank, and their contrasting opinions about the new building and its stages, while Bill Bryden shared his thoughts about the strong company he ran in the Cottesloe.

Also reprinted here are brief biographies of Federico García Lorca, Oscar Wilde, Philip Barry and Tennessee Williams, which I wrote as background to productions of *The House of Bernarda Alba*, *The Importance of Being Earnest*, *The Philadelphia Story* and *The Rose Tattoo*. I have also included a handful of reviews of theatre books that I wrote for the *Spectator*, the *Independent* and *Arts Express* magazine.

I have taken the opportunity to include four previously unpublished articles: an interview I had with the director Toby Robertson about the eventful history of the Prospect Theatre Company; a piece for which I talked to Peter Terson and the cast and company of his community play *Under the Fish and Over the Water*; a feature about the eccentric Ken Campbell's comedy workshop at the Royal Academy of Dramatic Art; and a record of my conversations with young playwrights involved in the Royal Court Young Writers' Festival.

These years spent working at the National and the Old Vic, giving me the chance to observe the British theatre at its very best, have been among the most satisfying of my writing career. I believe that giving the resulting pieces a more permanent life will provide a useful insight into the ideas and ways of working of some of our most talented actors and directors. I hope too that the collection will prove stimulating and informative, as well as occasionally entertaining, to anyone who shares my passion for the theatre.

Acknowledgements

I AM IMMENSELY GRATEFUL TO all the actors, directors and playwrights who allowed me to watch them at work, and to those who gave up their time to talk to me. The majority of the articles in this book appeared in publications I edited for the Old Vic and the National Theatre, and are reproduced by kind permission. Other pieces are reprinted by kind permission of the Ambassador Theatre Group (pages 95, 122, 131), Dewynters (page 152), *Arts Express* magazine (pages 181, 205), the *Spectator* (pages 207, 210, 213, 216) and *Independent* Print Ltd (page 215).

1

Classic Plays

A Moon for the Misbegotten – Bacchai – Gaslight –
The Women of Troy – The Philadelphia Story –
The Good Hope – Pygmalion

One Day's Journey

In the autumn of 2006 I spent an absorbing day watching an
Old Vic company rehearse A Moon for the Misbegotten. *At*
the end of the day the two leading players, Kevin Spacey and
Eve Best, and the director Howard Davies, talked to me
about working on Eugene O'Neill's powerful tragi-comedy.

CENTRE STAGE STANDS A SLIGHTLY tilted chipboard façade,
representing the Hogan farmhouse in Connecticut. Down
stage right is a low, rectangular chipboard box, standing in
for a big boulder on the estate. Like the set, the actors at this

early stage in rehearsals are also at the sketch stage, as they begin to shape the complex characters that drive O'Neill's powerful play.

We're in the large rehearsal room at the top of the Old Vic, where the company has been working for seven days under the gentle but firm guidance of director Howard Davies. Howard's method has been to get the actors on their feet quickly: last week they worked their way right through the play once, and this week they have returned to the first act to look at in detail.

The actors are at that awkward stage when they are half on and half off the book, making it hard for them to reproduce in any sustained way the complex thought-processes of their characters. Howard reminds them that their work will grow when they're able to look at each other more fully, and so feed off each other better.

Today they've moved on to Act 2, beginning with the scene between Hogan (Colm Meaney) and his daughter Josie (Eve Best), in which she learns of the apparent double betrayal by Jim Tyrone (Kevin Spacey). The actors are working from a script that at first glance seems heavily cut, but which turns out to have simply been shorn of O'Neill's detailed character profiles, redundant inflection suggestions and endless stage directions which, as Howard points out, can all too easily intimidate both director and actors.

In these first father-daughter skirmishes Colm and Eve combine effectively. Colm's very Irish energy, power and humour are soon in evidence, while Eve makes for a belligerent yet warm-hearted Josie. Howard gives them their head for several pages, enabling them to get into a rhythm and link several passages together, before he stops them to discuss their motivation and intentions.

When he does so, his aim is to pin down more precisely

the characters' many changes of thought and emotion. "It's a difficult scene, because there are all numbers of twists and turns," he suggests. "O'Neill has almost over-written it, but he's managed to cover all the bases. Hogan is feeding Josie information which she might or might not pick up. In fact she does so, which means that it is she who has to activate the story."

He and Eve discuss her hurt at being stood up by Tyrone, her feelings of shock at the sale of the estate, her anger with her father. He wants her initially to register a dull ache, but not yet her desire for revenge on Tyrone. When they run it again she does this more clearly. "Yes, so much better," Howard remarks. "I could see your hurt, and it made more sense, because you were just playing the moment, and not anticipating."

Alongside these discussions about the characters' inner life, practical details concerned with props and moves are not being neglected. Is the thick piece of wood standing in for a broom handle, with which Josie taps Hogan on the head, too heavy, and therefore a safety risk? Is it, Eve wonders, "too girlie" for the powerful Josie to hold it with two hands instead of one?

There are plenty of move changes from last time round, designed to alter the balance of power between the characters, or to inject an extra moment of humour. Among the latter is a suggestion from Howard that Colm in his drunken state should keel over on the steps and fall temporarily asleep. He does so, to good comic effect.

After lunch Kevin joins the rehearsal for Jim Tyrone's lengthy, emotion-packed scene with Josie. His skill at suggesting a long-time drunk is apparent from the moment he makes his entry. Through a deft combination of off-key movements, an unsteady stance, and a look that is alternately sharply focussed and far away, he manages to convey Tyrone's soused state without descending to cliché.

He and Eve have only worked once before on this scene, and over the afternoon session they experiment with different ways of playing its various components. It's a monumental challenge, for which O'Neill demands of the actors a bewildering mixture of despair, lust, pretence, honesty, cynicism, humour, cruelty and love.

Again they run the scene in large chunks, sometimes going ten minutes without a break. Some sections are still scratchy, others are really beginning to fly. As the feelings grow more intense, Kevin and Eve begin to get inside the skin of their roles, and find with precision the sequence of mood-swings. "You know how O'Neill's language works, so you're now really adding in the layers," Howard observes.

His style as a director is unshowy, but absolutely confident and precise. Although he's hot on detail, he avoids giving line readings. Just occasionally he will come out from behind his desk to emphasise an attitude he is looking for. He watches the actors' every move and gesture intensely, and is highly skilled at unravelling a story-line, or suggesting to the actors what's going on inside their characters' heads.

He and Eve talk about Josie's essential character, her honesty and openness, and how difficult it is – apart from her lies about her virginity – for her to simulate. He suggests that she bring in more of the back story of her earlier scene with her father, so that the nature of her hurt is clearer. "Much more complicated and interesting," he says, after she and Kevin have run the section once more.

The attempted rape scene is played with full, almost frightening force. "I should experiment with this idea, but I don't think at this moment he realises that it's Josie," Kevin says. "She's become every one of those girls from his past." In the subsequent passionate scene they keep the emotional pressure high, Eve somehow managing to kiss Kevin with convincing ardour while glancing at her script over his shoulder.

During a short break from this emotional roller-coaster there's a discussion about certain aspects of O'Neill's family life, in particular about his brother Jamie's involvement in their baby brother Edmond's death from measles. "Jamie was seven at the time: could it have been intentional?" Kevin wonders. "If not, he still must have had so much guilt afterwards."

The talk then moves on to Jamie's relationship with his mother, and his feelings about her death. This leads to one of those moments which occasionally occur in a rehearsal, when someone is prompted to share a key life-experience. On this occasion, both Howard and Kevin recall in detail different incidents following the deaths of their own mothers.

At the end of the day a lot of ground has been covered, and Howard is more than satisfied. After giving the actors some last detailed notes, he says: "We'll come back to all this on Friday, after we've done the next section again. You'll be able to colour that in, and you'll then see the whole journey."

Kevin Spacey / Jim Tyrone

JC Eugene O'Neill is obviously a playwright that means a lot to you. How did this come about?

KS I first was introduced to O'Neill when I was quite young. *Long Day's Journey* was the first play of his that I read, and it just hit me in the solar plexus. Then I started to read more of his plays and see some of them, and investigate those that were on film – Sidney Lumet's *Long Day's Journey*, Lee Marvin's *Iceman*, which is very rarely seen, and the TV version that Jason Robards did, in which Robert Redford played Don Parritt, and then this play.

The thing that you're looking for in any writer, and that continually stuns me when you come across it, is when they seem to have absolutely nothing that comes between their heart and the pen. Particularly in O'Neill's autobiographical work, whether it's *Iceman* or *Long Day's Journey* or *Moon*, he's able to write characters, including himself, at such a remarkable distance, and without seeming to have any judgement on them as people. He just presents them, warts and all. And by doing that, by being able to be that honest, and having that perspective, even on something that is obviously autobiographical when you read about O'Neill and his life, you understand what he was going through to write these plays, how painful and tortuous it was.

But in another way they're not biographical at all, because they've survived anyone having to have any knowledge about his life or his family or his experience. They have crystallised characters and experience in such a way that you don't have to know a thing about Eugene O'Neill, because you believe in the Tyrones in *Long Day's Journey*, you believe in those guys in that bar in *Iceman*. They are real characters, with all their complexities and contradictions.

O'Neill's interest to me has always been the struggle to escape from your past, and to be free in some way. I think all of his plays on a large level have these thematic foundations about forgiveness and redemption and seeking some kind of peace. And it's their struggles that end up making all of those characters worth paying attention to, worth experiencing and spending a few hours with.

JC What made you decide to do this play rather than say *Long Day's Journey*?

KS I'd already done *Long Day's Journey*. I played Jamie when I was 26 years old, in a production that Jonathan Miller directed on Broadway and at the Haymarket, with Jack Lemmon as James Tyrone. It was one of the very first big plays I did. I've played Hickey in *Iceman*, and there's no doubt that there's a lot of Jamie in Hickey, and a lot of Hickey in Jamie. I've always wanted to tackle *Moon*. It seemed the next logical step in terms of my own experience as an actor and what I wanted to do.

What drove him to write this play – which for some reason he came to loathe, but which I think is a minor masterwork – was his feeling that he hadn't been fair to his brother in *Long Day's Journey*, that he'd only told part of his story. He felt he owed his brother the opportunity to redeem himself, and to write a play that was about him later on. So I think *Moon* was his apology to his brother, for having made him such a shit in *Long Day's Journey*.

JC I'm struck having watched rehearsals this morning by the complexity and speed of the character's thought-processes. That must be a real challenge for an actor.

KS Yes, but it's also a challenge because of what you have to add to it. In the case of Jim Tyrone, there isn't a moment in this play when he isn't drunk or has been drinking. So you have to determine how you play a person who has been drinking for twenty-five years. How does the consumption of alcohol for a real honest-to-God alcoholic affect the way the brain works, what do you remember, where does your mind go?

It's quite clearly indicated in the text that there are moments when he doesn't know where he is. And then moments of incredible lucidity and honesty and clarity, with all the barney and the bullshit and the lies. So there is this other character, which is the drink. And when you're going to be on stage, for that long scene between him and Josie, how do you play that in such a way that it doesn't become monotonous, or have people think, Oh, we're just watching a drunk. It's easy to dismiss what someone says when you've not had a drink, so there are these levels: how do you start on them, how does he change, what does that drink do to him that the other drink didn't, where does he get to the point where he decides that he does want to confess what he desperately needs to confess?

JC I suppose it is early days yet, but are you feeling your way into that?

KS I probably won't do that until the end of Week 3. One of the things Howard does is stage the whole damn play in the first week. For some actors that is a startling thing, to be on your feet when you haven't any idea of what you're doing, but it actually gives you a foundation and a shape, which you can then use as a springboard for experimentation. I've got about the first two and a half acts in my head pretty much now, so I can put the book down. When you do that you can really start to deal with your partners as actors, to explore the meaning of what someone is doing, and the way that someone is saying the line to you that will alter and change what you might have thought the meaning was.

So I think over the next week, as I get the play more and more into my head, including that big confession, it will get a heck of a lot easier to start to explore the meaning and double-meanings and triple-meanings and all of the complexities and contradictions of the piece. And also the humour, because there's a lot of humour in it. People consider O'Neill tough or bleak, but I don't think it plays that way.

JC You mention Howard's method. What does he bring to you in rehearsal that you particularly value?

KS *Iceman* happened because Howard and I had unfinished business. When I was just starting out as an actor, Howard and Christopher Hampton were in New York with their production of *Les Liaisons Dangereuses*. I came in as a young actor to audition to replace Alan Rickman, and they decided I was the one they wanted. There was an actress they wanted as well, who was relatively known in the theatre, but not known as a famous star. When they presented us to the producers, the producers said "Who? We need names to sell tickets." And they were so in opposition that they decided to close the production, so it didn't continue with an American cast. It became quite a point of controversy. And I always remembered that Howard had held out for me.

So when I went to see a production of *Ivanov* at the Almeida, with Ralph Fiennes as Ivanov, I ended up spending an evening with Iain McDiarmid and Jonathan Kent, who were running the theatre. I must have told them that story, although I don't remember doing so, while we were discussing the possibility of my working at their theatre. I was so impressed with that *Ivanov*, it was beautifully well created, and I thought the Almeida would be a lovely place to work in. Three weeks later Jonathan called and said, "What about *Iceman Cometh*, with Howard Davies directing?" I went, "You fucker!" Because I loved O'Neill, I'd seen Jason Robards do the revival of it on Broadway in 1985. So I said yes.

And I remember walking into rehearsal the first day. I hadn't spent a lot of time on the play, I wanted to discover it with the company. And when we were in the middle of the read-through I looked around that room, and I looked at the actors who were cast, and I thought, Oh my God, he's just created the world. Howard works very well with groups of actors, and he does have a remarkable ability to create a world.

There is something that we have that I am lucky to have with a number of directors, and that is a kind of shorthand. He appreciates and sees O'Neill in the same terms as I do, although he will push me in certain directions, encourage me to go to certain places, and stop me being sentimental. It comes down to trust. Rhythmically we understand, or we think we understand, the intention of how things should come out.

O'Neill's characters are visceral, and the dialogue moves and shifts, and there's all that quick thinking – it requires a very quick mind to keep up with these characters. We also both of us believe very strongly in the idea that you never let the audience get ahead of you. That's why *Iceman* went by so fast: I talked like I was a rabbit being shot out of a cannon. There is just something about the way Howard approaches it, and the way he talks about it, that I am immediately able to grab on to. It gives me an anchor, so that if I am out there wandering in the dark waters, he is my anchor and dock. I know I can tie my boat up and I'll be all right.

JC I saw in the rehearsal this morning how good he is on detail.

KS They are all reminders, such as don't forget what that means, don't run over that line, what does that mean, close that out a little bit. He's quite specific about detail, and this kind of play is about detail, but detail of character. It's not an epic play with a lot to look at and a lot going on, although I think the accumulation of its parts makes it a kind of epic drama. But it's about people.

JC Do you find there is something special about playing at the Old Vic?

KS Absolutely. Part of it is the feeling you have in the building itself. Because this building has so much history to it, because so many greats have trod the stage, and made memorable evenings in theatre that people still talk about. Olivier did *Long Day's Journey* here, and everybody has worked on this stage; there's a spirit here, and it's the ghosts urging us on.

It is also acoustically the best theatre I've ever played in, hands down. It's better than any Broadway house, better than any other theatre, much better than the Almeida, which is a difficult house, even though it's only 180 seats, because you've got to get under that balcony, and over that balcony.

I have never lost my voice here. Sometimes it's rough, six or seven weeks into the run, but you can gauge it, and it comes right back at you. And I think it has to do with the horseshoe shape, you're not getting under or over a balcony, it just goes out, and you can actually place it. It feels remarkably more of an intimate theatre than its thousand seats would suggest. And I feel safe on it, I feel it's OK to go where the play asks me to go.

JC You were talking earlier about your admiration for Jason Robards.

KS I became very close to him towards the very end of his life. I had this wonderful conversation with him before he came to see *Iceman*, which I felt very honoured about. He said to me: "Listen, whenever you get stuck, and you think 'Oh shit, I can't fucking do this, I'll fail,' just lean back, and you'll feel a hand round the back of you, and that's O'Neill, and he'll just carry you through."

By a strange coincidence, he was the first actor to play Jamie on Broadway and I was the second. He turned *Iceman* into a gigantic hit when he first did it, and I did it later, and he turned *Moon* into a big hit in the 1970s with Josie Quintero, and now I'm doing it. We also, strangely enough, share a birthday, so I used to call him on July 26 and sing "Happy Birthday to Us", and he would say "Hey, kiddo." And when he came back stage when I was playing in *Iceman* in New York, he wasn't well; in fact he lived just another two years. He came back and said, "God, it's so good to see O'Neill alive and kicking." He was so pleased.

JC So all this is really fate.

KS I guess so. I wrote a piece for the *Times* when he died, which went into all that. I have a letter he sent me for opening night, which I had framed. It will probably end up over here in my dressing-room, because it just makes me smile.

Eve Best / Josie Hogan

JC What was the attraction to you of playing a woman whom O'Neill describes as a thirteen-stone hulk?

EB It's the most extraordinary part. The last big one I did was Hedda Gabler, and the main difference between her and Josie is that Josie is a nurturer and giver of life. She has the physical thing of working on the farm, and being in touch with something that has to do with promoting life and growing things and giving love, through her generosity and openness and all the best feminine qualities, of giving and nurturing and supporting and protecting and cherishing.

All of which Hedda denies in herself, cutting out any of

those instincts and rejecting them, all those qualities within her, so that she ends up destroying herself. So it's wonderful to be presented with a part like this, and the fact that she is so honest and straightforward. She's a farmer, she has to get up at dawn, and deal with the pigs and the hay and the horses, so you don't have time to worry about yourself, you're dealing with the earth, and not your own neuroses. I found that very attractive and wonderful, the opportunity to explore that, in contrast to Hedda.

JC I can see from the rehearsal that the changes of thought and mood are very tricky to get hold of.

EB I was really struggling with it today, and a lot of it comes with not being on top of the direction of the scene. But sometimes it's rather wonderful, because you're going in one direction, and you suddenly find yourself going in a completely different one, and you can't do the knitting in between.

What Howard was so brilliant at in *Mourning Becomes Electra* and also now in *Moon* is being on top of the language as it happens, not pre-empting what will happen as you go through the changes. The writing is doing it for you I suppose. He talks about it being visceral, not just visceral as you're experiencing things physically, but the way also you experience the language physically, and so there's not too much off-line stuff. Particularly with Josie, who is a very honest person, who when she feels something just comes out with it, but now she has to be duplicitous.

JC Can you draw on your experience of *Mourning Becomes Electra*, even though it's a very different play?

EB I thought at the time it was the hardest thing I've ever done. I've now completely revised my opinion. *Hedda* also seemed the hardest at the time, but this play makes *Hedda* seem like a walk in the park. It's physically exhausting, so there has to be a robustness to it. I feel a similarity, but it's a much more complex play than *Mourning*, which at the time seemed hard. But now I look back on it, it seems very clear, because it was plot driven, so it was A to B to C, it was fairly straightforward once you had worked it out, because the feelings were quite clearly set out. *Moon* is much more complicated, because it's about characters, and this relationship between Josie and Tyrone, and the way they feel about each other. The plot seems to be a device just to get them to the situation where they can confront each other.

JC From what I've seen so far, your accent sounds very authentic.

EB If so, that's good. I've had a couple of sessions with our dialect coach Joan Washington, who is brilliant. When she first told me about the accent I was confused, because it's half Irish and half American, and not an accent I've heard before. I don't have any reference for it. But getting the accent right is not just about that, it's about attitude, because the shapes of the words in your mouth give you a different energy, so Irish is very different from received pronunciation, it's much more out there.

JC How does Howard help you as a director?

EB He's one of my favourite directors. He's completely brilliant with the text, he sees so clearly what's going on, and manages to make very clear to you what's going on inside somebody's head. He also has the most amazing instincts for what works and what doesn't, and if something is going all right he'll let it run, and if it's stuck, he'll rescue you. He's very generous, he gives a lot. He's also completely bullshit-free, it's so straight, it's all about getting the story down.

Within the first day we were already up on our feet, the

following day we'd blocked it. No mucking about. I came in the first day absolutely petrified. We did a read-through, then we were straight up on our feet. You're straight in there, so there's no time to worry or get stuck going down little alleyways. You've just got to do it, and it's tough, it's really hard work. Like all brilliant directors you respect, you want to do your best for them. It's like training for the pentathlon, you need your trainer, and I totally trust him.

JC How have you felt about working with Kevin?

EB Absolutely marvellous. It's like getting to dance the first steps. It's fabulous, I love it, because there's lots of playing around, which I really like. It means you can go to all kinds of places, and you're really responding to each other, and not being stuck thinking, "How are we going to do this?" That's when it's great, and it means rehearsals are really stimulating.

JC I can see that you've already reached quite an intensity of feeling.

EB I felt I was all over the place today, frankly, although the script seems to be very clear about what is happening. I certainly feel I haven't got there in terms of what's going on inside me being properly projected. I know that at that point I have to be broken down into tears, and I can do that even though I'm still holding the script and I'm not ready to go there. So those bits are more straightforward than the earlier bits to do with plotting. Kissing and holding the script always makes me laugh.

I've always wanted to do something that is a really big challenge. Apart from the fact that she's totally different from Hedda and very strong, the other thing about Josie is that she's second-generation Irish-American, a tinker, a farmer's daughter, and just a completely different character to me, a different physicality, different accent, different life experience. The only thing we share is the lack of confidence about the way we look. So I try to find all that stuff and play these complicated emotional scenes, and get the story right and get the accent right, and try to learn a whole new way, and how she responds so differently to how I would respond.

Howard Davies / Director

JC What's the particular fascination for you of O'Neill's plays?

HD The fact that they are big and raw and epic. He seems to be struggling with very big, fundamental themes: love and betrayal, and the sense of people carving out their destiny, but being trapped by their own human frailty, trying to rise above it but usually failing. Then being caught up in the consequences of betrayal or revenge or love that goes sour, and a sense of guilt.

All these things are really big, but they're very human and totally recognisable. I'm much more interested in plays that deal with that, and O'Neill's certainly do, than dealing with people sitting in a sitting-room being angst-ridden. Contemporary drama is usually so small and middle-class and neurotic. That bores me witless. Other people have got their hands on the rights for Tennessee Williams and Arthur Miller because they're slightly more accessible, but they avoid O'Neill because they think he's difficult or clunky in his language, or that the themes overwhelm the characters. I think they're wrong to avoid him. I think he's fantastic.

JC This must be a very different experience from directing *Mourning Becomes Electra*.

HD It is, because it's not a play that is plot driven.

There is a plot, there's a revenge plot of a kind, but it's a fantastically complicated one. Josie Hogan is going to seduce the man she loves in order to get revenge on him. She feels that he's betrayed both her emotionally and her father and herself economically by selling the farm that they live on, which he had promised to her. That means that she is going to get Jim Tyrone into bed in order to blackmail him, because with her sense of her low self-esteem she only sees herself as being big and ugly, and that he would be shamed by announcing publicly his handing the farm back to them or handing them money.

Moon is really about character, whereas *Mourning* is a melodrama, which is absolutely about the plot. In a Greek way you know what's going to happen, there's not a question in that which doesn't already tell you what's going to happen. And sure enough the process of the play is to watch with some kind of anxiety and awe as the plot which you know unfolds. Usually you and one or two of the characters know what's going to happen, and you watch while a third person is practised upon – murdered, killed.

In *Moon* you have no knowledge of what's going to unfold, and whether this rather wonderful character Josie will stop abasing herself, and find in or believe in herself that she has the germ of some rare beauty or grace. And whether Jim, who also runs himself down and thinks himself unlovable and guilty of betraying his mother's love, whether he will be redeemed, and find that he can forgive himself. So instead of treating her like a lover he ends up treating her like a mother, because she is able to forgive him, and replace the maternal forgiveness that he's sought.

They do manage to give each other what each other needs, but it's not in a conventional sexual way. And it's much more about generosity – surprisingly enough he's very generous about her, given that he's somewhat of a cynic. And she's fantastically forgiving of him, even though he's revealed himself to be quite ugly on an emotional level. That trading between the two of them allows them both to find something else. We know historically that O'Neill is writing an elegy and a lament for his own brother, that in 1943 he's writing autobiographically about his own past. He's wrestling with his family again, but on this particular occasion he goes back, and in the process of the writing manages to forgive his brother for what he was and did.

JC Watching you at work this morning, I'm struck by the characters' complex and swift changes of mood and thought. That's quite a challenge for a director, isn't it?

HD It is, and that's part of what he's good about, he just goes screeching round corners. He doesn't take you there in an inexorable way. It's not subtle writing in the sense that you suddenly find yourself facing a completely different position in the way that you now see this character. You've got there by who knows what means. It's not invisibly or subtly done, he's not a card-sharper in that way. He just goes black one minute, white the next, bang, bang! So when the actors are required to turn on a sixpence it is either crude or, with dextrous acting, it will look fantastically thrilling, because it will be an emotional somersault.

JC Talking of dextrous acting, what do you think you can give Kevin in particular?

HD The actors who are really brilliant have got a very odd third eye on both the play and their own acting. It's a quality that you don't find very often in American actors, because most of them don't believe you should have a third eye, whereas there is a belief among stage actors in Britain that you should have one, that you're responsible both to the play and to the rest of the cast as well as to your own character, that you carry a double responsibility. I think most of the American training is to do with the Method school, and because it's a film rather than a theatre culture, you are cast for that role and you are only responsible for that role, because God knows what's going to happen in the editing.

So people don't have that quality, but Kevin has it big time. He can see objectively as well as play subjectively. So I don't have to talk about the subjective nature of what he's doing, I can say, "No you can't do that there, because" – and before I've finished the sentence it's, "I've got it." He knows where I'm coming from as a director. So there's a shorthand which is about him recognising what I'm trying to do, it's about him coming across the line to me.

It's interesting, I can give him a complicated note such as, "The second time around you played that line emotionally, it was about your own emotions. The first time around was better, when you told Josie she was big and beautiful and strong, you gave her all the values, so it was very generous, and it's better." And he just goes, "Oh okay." Some actors with a note like that will say "Why is it better?" because they're not standing outside. That's not a fault, it's just not being able to see objectively why that would work better for the storytelling of the play. But Kevin gets it straight away.

JC It was interesting that you cast Eve Best as Josie Hogan, as she obviously doesn't fit the physical description of her in the text.

HD I've only worked with Eve once before, on *Mourning Becomes Electra*. Knowing that she could cope with O'Neill's ability to slam the brakes on and make incredible turns and twists, because she did it brilliantly in *Mourning*, I thought that's what I really need. The physicality of the part, the fact that she's not big, was less important than her attitude in the acting. It's like age. All those guys who played *Iceman* with Kevin were all far too young to be playing the parts they had, as he was. But it didn't matter: if you tell a story well enough, that's what counts.

From the Olivier to Epidaurus

In 2002 I was writing a book about Peter Hall's National Theatre production of Euripides' Bacchai. *While he was rehearsing the play for a run in the Olivier, I recorded his thoughts about working in the open-air theatre at Epidaurus in Greece. Once we were there, I watched the actors working right through until dawn, preparing to perform this classic play in the world-famous home of Greek drama.*

A Most Holy Place

PETER HALL IS IN NO doubt about the stature of the play he is now rehearsing at the National. "*Bacchai* is one of the most original plays ever written, and certainly in the top dozen of all time. Whenever it's performed it seems to be extraordinarily timely."

After its run in the Olivier, his production of *Bacchai* will travel to Greece, where in June it will open the Athens Festival as part of the Cultural Olympiad. There Colin Teevan's version of Euripides' powerful blood-stained tragedy, with designs by Alison Chitty, will be staged in masks at Epidaurus.

It's a theatre that Hall knows intimately, having directed eight productions there in the last twenty years, including

Aeschylus' *The Oresteia*, Sophocles' *Oedipus Rex* and *Oedipus at Colonus*, Aristophanes' *Lysistrata*, and Shakespeare's three "late plays", *Cymbeline*, *The Tempest* and *The Winter's Tale*. "It still feels like what it was originally, a place of healing," he says. "It's the most holy place an actor can go to, set in the middle of the countryside. You talk to the gods, and there's the sky; you talk to the underworld, and there's the earth. The acoustics are amazing: you're playing to ten thousand people, who can hear every word without you needing to shout. It's an extraordinary place.

"When we did *The Oresteia* there in 1981, the fact that we did it with an all-male cast, and in masks, absolutely amazed the Greeks. Their tradition then was based more on the theatre spectacle of Max Reinhardt than anything Greek. Things have changed to some extent since, but there's still a tradition that the Chorus wear masks and the stars don't. Personally I don't think you can mix the two.

"Some of the older Greek actors were extremely affronted that we did Shakespeare at Epidaurus. In their view the ancient theatres should only do ancient plays. We got a special dispensation, but they were furious. This modern upstart Shakespeare!"

Euripides Comes Home

Epidaurus. 7pm, 26 June 2002. At the end of the path leading up through the woods to the stage, the actors are confronted with a breathtaking sight. There in front of them, in the fading light, is the elegant auditorium of the ancient theatre, a curve of limestone carved into the hillside, where 2,400 years ago their predecessors acted out the ancient stories of the Greek drama.

As they prepare to start rehearsing, the actors spread out into the theatre and the auditorium, absorbing the atmosphere. Several of them gather round the stone that is set in the middle of the stage area, said to be sacred, and reputedly used in ancient times for animal sacrifices A couple of them test the celebrated acoustics, standing on the stone and speaking lines in an ordinary voice that can be heard with absolute clarity at the top of the auditorium. From the top of the 108 rows of stone seating there is a fine view of the distant mountains, and the hills dotted with olive groves.

Nine hours later a pale light from the East begins to sharpen the edge of the mountains. Around the plane covered with pine trees, olive groves and vineyards a chorus of birds stirs into song. Meanwhile, on the circle of bare earth on the hillside, a very different Chorus struggles to fight off sleep. As dawn steals over the ancient theatre, the dress-rehearsal for *Bacchai* is nearing its end.

Halfway up the amphitheatre, sitting on the limestone steps which seem to rise up to touch the sky, the familiar figure of Peter Hall becomes visible. Through the night, microphone in hand, he has been struggling with his sound and lighting teams to overcome the formidable technical problems of performing in this vast theatrical space. The actors and musicians are exhausted: for two nights they have been rehearsing Euripides' tragedy into the early hours. The design of the Olivier theatre, the scene of their successful London run, was based on Epidaurus. This is the real thing: the play is coming home.

In a few hours the production will open the Epidaurus Festival, one of two parallel strands of the Hellenic Festival (the other takes place in Athens). Now in its forty-seventh year, the festival is devoted to staging the major ancient Greek tragedies and comedies. This summer sees ten plays by Aristophanes, Euripides, Sophocles and Aeschylus playing over the July and August weekends. The programme includes the world premiere of Euripides' *Hypsipile*, which has been pieced together from fragments.

The Greeks welcome foreign productions of their classics. "This theatre belongs not only to Greece, but to the universe," says Periklis Koukos, the festival's artistic director. "We are always keen to remain open to modern trends and interpretations of these brilliant texts."

Set in the Argolid countryside in the Eastern Peloponnese, with Mount Arachnaio in the distance, Epidaurus is the best-preserved of all the theatres surviving from the ancient world. Built in the fourth century BC, it can hold up to fourteen thousand people, although a running programme of repairs means that ten thousand is now effectively the maximum. Audiences tend to be two-thirds Greek, one third foreign visitors, with the latter increasing in number. The auditorium spans more than 180 degrees, enveloping the central stage area, and posing a formidable challenge to actors needing to involve the whole audience.

The theatre's harmony and elegance are breathtaking, its acoustics astonishing.

The actors are intimidated, exhilarated and moved by playing here. Despite its size, they find it a surprisingly intimate theatre, due perhaps in part to its steep incline. They speak also of the deeply calm atmosphere of the place, and the weight of dramatic history hanging heavy on their shoulders. One actor, taking a nap in the nearby dressing rooms, swears he had a momentary vision of an old actor with a white beard smiling down on him.

Traditionally performances at Epidaurus cannot start until the sun has set over the mountain. Tonight, the audience – some eight thousand strong – walk up through the woods in the gathering dusk, to come face-to-face with the huge auditorium. Peter Hall hovers in a corner with his family, watching the stone seats steadily fill with colour and human form. "All the work I've done on the Greeks has been informed by this place," he says. "Of all the ancient theatres that I know, this one seems to me the most alive and sympathetic."

Hall is widely admired in Greece. Having staged eight productions in twenty years at Epidaurus – including Aeschylus' *The Oresteia* and Sophocles' *The Oedipus Plays* – his status here is almost godlike. "It's because he deeply respects our drama," Periklis Koukos says. "To us Peter Hall is an Ancient Greek." As Hall walks to his seat the audience marks his arrival with fervent and sustained applause.

Dusk settles, and Dionysos (in the shape of Greg Hicks) walks into the circle. "An empty space, and all of you, and me." The play begins, and for the next two hours, under a darkening sky and backed by the sound of nightjars and crickets, Euripides' complex tragedy unfolds. The company's compelling performance holds the attention of the audience throughout.

I watched the play from near the top of the auditorium, from where the theatre below seems like a bowl of light set in the Greek countryside. To witness such a potent spectacle in such a setting is an overwhelming experience, and one of which the gods would surely approve.

Peter Hall was certainly satisfied: "I think that's the best work the company have yet done on the play," he says as we leave the theatre. "They used the energy of the thousands of people out front, and drew something extra from this extraordinary place. They were pretty magnificent."

More than Spooky

At the end of a long but fruitful day's work at the Old Vic, director Peter Gill and leading players Rosamund Pike, Kenneth Cranham and Andrew Woodall shared with me their enthusiasm for Patrick Hamilton's thriller Gaslight, *and spoke of its unexpected complexity.*

IT'S THE BEGINNING OF THE second week of rehearsals. In the rehearsal room in the Old Vic, the Victorian period is already much in evidence. A pile of nineteenth-century novels is stacked up on a table. On a wall are pictures from the time – Walter Sickert, Atkinson Grimshaw – showing shadowy or rain-washed London streets. In the middle of the room the set is gradually evolving, the focus a table covered in a rich coloured cloth, on which is laid a delicate china tea set.

Director Peter Gill, having set the production in 1880, has spent much of the first week easing the actors into the period. He's encouraged them to examine and speak the poetry of Tennyson, Kipling and Matthew Arnold, to consider the sexual politics of the era, and to look at attitudes to notions such as deference which characterised the time. Now, at the end of a hard day's work, he and the three principals in his production talk enthusiastically about Patrick Hamilton's thriller, and the demands of their roles in it.

"I saw it years ago at Windsor Rep, and was riveted by it," Peter recalls. "It's a good story and very well-written. I don't want to make more claims for it than the writer would, but I do think that there is hidden inside it a play about the middle-class male fantasy of the working-class girl and the middle-class wife, which Hamilton might have developed had there not been a Lord Chamberlain."

The actors are clearly fascinated by the play. "I find it very intriguing, because it has a great oddness to it, but also some poetic beauty," Kenneth Cranham says. "There are passages where what you know about Hamilton and his life seeps through." Andrew Woodall is similarly impressed. "I find it sinister for lots of different reasons, and the more we work on it, the more unnerving it is. It has a reputation of being a spooky play, but it's a lot more shocking than that: it's a psychologically interesting play about wife abuse."

Rosamund Pike, who confesses to being a great fan of Hamilton's novels, thinks *Gaslight* plays much better than it reads. "On the page it can look hideously old-fashioned, full of hokum and creaking plot mechanics," she suggests. "But when you start working on it and playing with the writing, you realise there is a lot of insidious stuff going on, and that it's a wonderfully witty and structured play."

Peter is famous for his encyclopaedic knowledge, which he invariably uses to drop in information that can stimulate a new thought, or a different angle on a character. All three actors find this invaluable: "He's got a library in his head, and he likes to share it," Andrew observes. Kenneth adds: "I've never asked him a question that he's been unable to answer." They also welcome his insistence on precision, on keeping them punctiliously to the surprisingly complex text, and ensuring the meaning is made absolutely clear.

Each of the main roles presents a different challenge for the actor. Andrew, playing Mr Manningham, has played his share of villains over the years, among them a pederast, a wife-beater, and bastard Edmund in *King Lear*. For him, the main question so far is whether the satanic husband is an unmitigated villain. "It's a knock-out part, but he doesn't really have any redeeming features. On the other hand I think when he says he might have been an actor, that's genuine. There's a kind of horrible innocence about him, and he's also slightly pathetic. But I think at the moment that you just have to play him as a complete sadist."

Rosamund, who gave such a memorable performance last year as Miss Alma in Tennessee Williams' *Summer and Smoke*, clearly relishes taking on another character of an extreme nervous sensibility. "Mrs Manningham is a very complex woman living in a very narrow world. It's a real nightmare for her, imagining that she's going mad, but having no outward reality to judge whether she is or not. She's imprisoned in her own head, without having anyone to confide in or to reassure her, so when the detective Rough comes in he's like her guardian angel. She's a very intense character, who has the potential to give love and affection. Her spirit isn't crushed, which I think is really important. Otherwise the audience would give up on her, instead of rooting for her."

Kenneth has played a succession of policeman in his career, most notably nearly eight hundred performances as Inspector Goole in Stephen Daldry's celebrated revival of Priestley's *An Inspector Calls*. As ex-detective Rough he calls again, but as a very different character in very different circumstances. "It's a challenging role, because you don't get parts of this substance any more," he says. "He's a complicated character, and you don't quite know who he is, or quite what he's up to. I imagine him as a dedicated policeman who was made to retire, and it's something he can't stop doing. I think he's got a housekeeper, but not a wife: he's one of those career men. But even though he's just a policeman, he's fantastically articulate."

Many people will know *Gaslight* only through the two screen versions, the 1944 American one directed by George Cukor with Ingrid Bergman and Charles Boyer being better known than the 1940 British film, starring Diana Wynyard and Anton Walbrook.

Peter observes that neither is faithful to the play. "It's very odd, they're so frightened it won't be a film, so they give it a back story, which means it's an age before they get to the story proper. In both cases they felt the husband had to be foreign – and yet this is a Patrick Hamilton story, it's about a typically English deviant. And they set the film in houses in squares, which was much too grand: they should have been in a place such as Waterloo or Islington or Kensington."

Both Kenneth and Andrew have seen the American film, but Rosamund has refrained from doing so. For research purposes she has found it useful to watch other films: *The Elephant Man*, for an insight into Victorian attitudes, and Hitchcock's *Rebecca*, where she sees parallels with *Gaslight*: "There's the same feeling about a house that's terrifying, and the young wife's desperate need to please."

It's time to clock off for the day. Ahead lie three weeks of intense rehearsal, under Peter's stimulating direction. No doubt the company will be delving deeper into Patrick Hamilton's absorbing piece of theatre, which has continued to intrigue audiences for nearly seventy years.

Original and Controversial

Katie Mitchell's distinctive productions invariably provoke strong reactions. In the autumn of 2007 two actors involved in her production of Euripides' Women of Troy *at the National talked to me about the process she takes them through.*

WITH DIRECTOR KATIE MITCHELL'S PRODUCTIONS you learn to expect the unexpected. In recent years she has created a series of provocative and iconoclastic productions at the National which have severely divided critics and audiences.

They include a new version of Chekhov's *The Seagull*; a radical take on Strindberg's notoriously difficult *Dream Play*; a multi-media adaptation of Virginia Woolf's novel, renamed *Waves*; and a revisiting of Martin Crimp's complex play *Attempts on her Life*. There was also Euripides' *Iphigenia at Aulis*, now to be followed by another of his War Plays, *Women of Troy*, which seems likely to prove equally original and controversial.

In this masterpiece of Greek drama, set at the end of the ten-year Trojan War, Euripides focuses on the tragic situation of Hecuba, Andromache, Cassandra and other women, as their beloved Troy goes up in flames, and they are taken away to become slaves or concubines of the conquering Greek soldiers. Because of its powerful anti-war sentiments, the play seems to resonate for every age, whether it's being staged in 1918 in support of the fledgling League of Nations, or played against a backdrop of wars in Iraq and Afghanistan in 2007.

Katie Mitchell's basic aim in approaching a classic is to clarify it for a modern audience. While working at the National on Aeschylus' *The Oresteia*, she made this explicit: "It's the form which is a real challenge for a director. It's like having a car you've never driven before, and you've got to dismantle it, put it back together again with the actors, and see if it will move." On that occasion she was working with Ted Hughes' version of the play, which she described as having a "very direct, simple, happening-in-the-kitchen style of writing that hits you between the eyeballs". With *Women of Troy* she is using a cut-down version of playwright Don Taylor's powerful and modern translation, in which he has chosen to omit the characters of the Gods.

As with her earlier productions, her interpretation of *Women of Troy* will be based on extensive research and a unique rehearsal process. As is normal, rehearsals have been preceded by a week's workshop at the National's Studio, where a group of actors (not necessarily the final cast) has been exploring the director's initial concept and playing around with ideas within it. Michael Gould, who plays the Greek officer Talthybius, recalls a major strand of the workshop:

"We experimented with a twenty-first-century setting, and discussed the idea of departure lounges, those bland, faceless places at ports or airports. We looked at the idea of deportation: who are the people who administer it, what do they feel when they're deporting someone with whom they may have an affinity, which might clash with their official duty? And where does that leave them emotionally or politically or morally?"

This kind of work has led to a decision to set the play "in an industrial port of a war-torn city". Rehearsals, which begin shortly, will be very different from the traditional sequence of read-through, blocking, and then working on scenes. First the actors discuss the themes of the play, establish the concrete facts present in the text, list the questions they feel need to be answered, and start to build up their characters' biography, looking at their back story. Throughout this process, which continues right through rehearsals, they use improvisation as a tool for exploration.

"We might take the theme of grief, and look at how that has been present in our own lives," explains Anastasia Hille, who is playing Andromache. "We take a situation and then a character, and improvise around them, so that eventually we have a set of improvisations that give us a corporate history of each character. We are all involved, trying to understand what grief means to each of us."

In her two most recent productions – *Waves* and *Attempts on her Life* – Katie Mitchell, an associate at the National, has introduced video and other media. This has meant that the actors have had to learn additional skills. Michael Gould recalls his initial terror when starting *Waves*: "I said to Katie, 'You're asking me to do everything I can't do, like tap dancing and Foley sound effects, and nothing I can do; I shall have to reconfigure myself.' But I'm glad I did, because it was very liberating. By the end I felt I could think of myself not just as an actor but as a performance artist."

As well as these demands, the actors have to be prepared to take away "homework", and bring it in the following day. This rigorous and thorough process clearly demands a certain sort of temperament. "Those who have worked with Katie over a long period tend to be quite self-effacing people, very flexible and willing, very open to experiment," Anastasia Hille suggests. "They're very interested in the form and structure of the production; they focus on being a piece within a picture, because the picture is what interests them."

Many of the *Women of Troy* cast are regulars in her productions, which makes for something of a company feel. "It's a great advantage working with people you are already familiar with," Michael Gould says. "It's a notably generous group that she gathers around her, so you can lean on each other and trust each other, know where individuals are coming from, and what aspects of the play they might be drawn to."

Anastasia Hille believes this set-up gives the actors more security. "You go a bit deeper early on if you've known the others a long time. Because some of us have done a lot of shows together, there's a shorthand, and an amazing bond between people." She denies the suggestion that this might turn into a clique, that excludes or at least intimidates newcomers. "It doesn't become exclusive," she says. "When someone new comes along, they blend in and create an exciting dynamic."

For these two actors and others, what attracts them to work with Katie Mitchell is the knowledge that they will be active partners in a rich creative process, a fact that was reflected publicly in the programme credit for *Attempts on her Life*, which read: "Directed by Katie Mitchell and the Company".

Coming into Focus

In the summer of 2005 I spent two days observing the American director Jerry Zaks putting together his production at the Old Vic of Philip Barry's The Philadelphia Story, *with the help of a cast that included Kevin Spacey, Jennifer Ehle, Nicholas le Prevost and Julia Mackenzie.*

DAY 8 OF REHEARSALS. A large room at the top of the Old Vic. A rough set is marked out on the floor; on it are pieces of antique furniture. Here, under the skilful guidance of their director, the actors are refining and polishing Act 1 of Philip Barry's popular classic.

Jerry Zaks is a big name on Broadway, with four Tonys among his many awards. Lively and energetic, casually dressed in jeans and checked shirt, he's already creating a relaxed atmosphere in the rehearsal room. "I want the actors to feel safe, and to trust me," he explains. "When they first get up on their feet they are vulnerable to being embarrassed, and as soon as that happens they will shut down. But the moment they feel it's okay to make mistakes, the more daring they will be."

His style is to mix positive feedback ("All good, my dears") and valuable insights with a smattering of gags. He frequently comes onto the set to discuss a thought with an actor, or to suggest and demonstrate a new move or action. He loves to plant ideas, experiment with alternatives: "Let's see what happens" is a regular expression.

The actors have now set aside their scripts, and the opening section introducing the Lord family is beginning to flow, with Julia McKenzie's neat comic timing already in evidence. From the start Jerry shows a sharp eye for the overall visual picture, especially when there are many characters on stage. "We need to be clear who is looking at whom, so the whole audience's attention is focused on one place," he says.

Often he will take an actor aside and give them a private note. "I made it clear from the start that I would be doing this," he says. "It's partly because if I give them a public note, there's a lot of pressure on them to come up with the goods straight away, whereas if no one knows what I'm saying, it's less threatening. It also enables me to suggest they do something completely different, and then see how the other actors react to it."

A simple change can radically alter the shape of a scene, and unlock new possibilities. Until now Nicholas le Prevost (Uncle Willy) has made his first entrance from stage right, and remained there. But he's not certain this is right for his character at that moment. Jerry is initially uncertain about making a change, but when another actor quietly suggests one to him, he agrees to bring Nicholas into the centre. The scene is transformed.

In the afternoon, after further detailed work, the

company runs through the first act up to the moment of Dexter's entrance. Some sections are very funny, but others seem to have lost a little momentum. A second run-through is sharper and tighter. "That's a good first draft," Jerry says. "Now we'll leave it alone for a week or two."

Unlike some directors, he doesn't hesitate to correct line readings. As the actors leave, he explains why: "Sometimes an actor says a line that has nothing to do with their character's choices at that moment. They may also stress words arbitrarily. Actors are craftsmen in the same way that members of a symphony orchestra are craftsmen. If I'm a conductor, I'm not going to have any qualms about telling a musician 'There's no rest there' or 'That's a half note, so play it as a half note'. Of course you have to be careful, as some actors don't like you to do this, they say it makes them self-conscious. But if the note is intrinsically valuable, there's plenty of time to get over that in rehearsal."

Day 9. On to Act 2. The actors are back on their scripts: this is the first time they've been on their feet with these scenes. "We'll stumble our way through," Jerry says.

They begin at the point where Tracy (Jennifer Ehle) and Mike (D. W. Moffett) are alone for the first time. The challenge here is to unravel how their feelings for each other are developing, or not. Is she attracted to him, or just impressed that he can write short stories as well as hack journalism? How far is he put off by her failure to understand that writers need to eat, or by her patronising of him? After considerable discussion the two of them try the scene in different ways. "Now it begins to make sense," Jerry says. "Because the intentions are clear, there's no inappropriate subtext."

During a break he stresses his desire to be flexible. "I want the actors to know that not all my notions are right, but I'm open to other people's suggestions, because often they can improve on mine. I used to come in with the moves all worked out, because I hated not having an answer. I realise now that I don't have to be quite so meticulous. As long as I have a sense of what's happening in the scene, and at the end of the day review it in my mind and decide what worked and what didn't, that usually serves."

The actors now start on the central scene of the play, in which Dexter (Kevin Spacey) tells Tracy some home truths about her character. "We need to work out how toe-to-toe this scene should get," Jerry says. "This is the first time that someone has told her that she is not what she thinks she is." Kevin plays it on the wing, trusting his instincts, moving when it seems right to do so, laughing at unexpected moments, throwing certain lines away.

For the moment it's clearly all fluid: when they go over the scene twice more, he moves at different moments to different places, is serious where previously he was funny, becomes predatory where before he played light-hearted. Jennifer seems unfazed by this unpredictability. Responding calmly to whatever he comes up with, she conveys with increasing subtlety the ambiguity of Tracy's feelings for Dexter. Kevin remarks: "I love the idea of it being so open at this stage."

In the final hour Jennifer and Richard Lintern work on the tender scene between Tracy and her fiancé George, in which he reveals his intention of worshipping her like a goddess. Jerry observes: "All George's lines here are one line, and that is, I love you, I love you." The two actors, who have quickly found a natural ease and intimacy in the scene, experiment with Jerry's suggestions for alternative positions and movements. Jennifer ends up sitting on the sofa, with

Richard at her feet, the tableau neatly symbolising their relationship.

It's a pleasing end to a very satisfying day. The actors have had the freedom to experiment, while Jerry has helped them to find the essence of their scenes, and precise motivations for their characters. As they break for the last time, Jerry tells them: "It's coming into focus. I think this is going to lead to something really good."

Sounds Gorgeous

In the winter of 2001 a new version by Lee Hall of the Dutch classic The Good Hope *was staged at the National before going on tour. The musician John Tams talked to me about how music played a key part in the Cottesloe production.*

THE DUTCH HAVE REALLY ONLY got two classic plays, the miracle play *Jederman*, and this famous story by Herman Heijermans, set in a fishing village. It's a very political piece, tragic but also funny.

Fifteen years ago I worked with Bill Bryden on a production in Rotterdam. For the National one Bill and I talked about setting it in East Anglia. But we felt that the voice was a little soft, that the Yorkshire voice was more robust and would give it more edge. So we set it in Whitby on the east coast. Lee Hall, who has written this version, is from Newcastle, so he knows the musicality of the region's language.

I wanted the bonding factor to be community singing with strong, vernacular voices. One of the things that gets overlooked about the human voice is that it's the only instrument in the world that can do two things at once. It can do music, and break your heart with a story.

The musicians play acoustic vernacular instruments, and come on as characters. One instrument I wanted to use was a hammered dulcimer, which has a gorgeous sound not widely heard, but very typical of the east coast. The musician I found is also a champion clog dancer, so it became obvious that there had to be a celebratory clog dance.

Much of the production is based on the work of Frank Meadow Sutcliffe, the great Victorian photographer. We've taken his shot of a one-man band and made it a two-man band, one with a bass drum and an accordion, the other a blind banjo player. They're tethered together, which makes it funny, but also eerie and rather sad.

I also wanted English pipes, another sound the audience won't often have met, except in the Scots and Irish vernacular. They're Border pipes, which are sweeter than Northumbrian pipes. They make a really nice buzzy sound, like organised bees in a bottle – if you can get them organised enough and keep the lid on.

Suiting the Thought to the Word

In the spring of 2008 I caught up with Peter Hall and an Old Vic company in a rehearsal for Shaw's popular classic Pygmalion, *which starred Tim Pigott-Smith as Henry Higgins and Michelle Dockery as Eliza Doolittle.*

IN A LARGE, LIGHT AND elegant room behind Chelsea Old Church, with the April sunlight pouring through the window, the rehearsal is about to begin. Under director Peter Hall's expert guidance it promises to be a full and varied one, covering key scenes in Professor Higgins' laboratory in Wimpole Street and his mother's flat on the

Chelsea Embankment, and giving all the principal actors a chance to take centre stage.

Although this is only the company's third day of rehearsal here, the production is already well established. By the time it opens at the Old Vic it will have played more than a hundred performances. It began last year as one of the plays in the Peter Hall Company's summer residency at the Theatre Royal in Bath. It then went on a nine-week UK tour, and will have two further weeks of touring before arriving in the Waterloo Road for a three-month visit.

So there are no scripts in sight, no need to spend time working out basic moves, deciding on props, or getting used to the set. Instead the actors have the bonus of additional time to explore the play more fully. As the morning progresses, it's clear they already have a deep understanding of their characters and the text.

They start at the end of Act 2. Mrs Pearce the housekeeper has been complaining to Higgins about his bad language and slovenly manners. Tim Pigott-Smith is a boisterous, mercurial Higgins, full of energy – which he needs to be, as he is on stage virtually all the time. An early question is how he should play the line, "I'm a shy, diffident sort of man." Does he mean it? Is he being ironic? And how should Pickering (an urbane and sympathetic James Laurenson) react to this surprising news?

Enter Alfred Doolittle, spokesman for "the undeserving poor". Tony Haygarth makes a convincingly earthy dustman, humorously putting over the likeable shrewdness of Shaw's great character. Peter suggests a slightly different "colouring" for the odd phrase or two, which Tony then plays around with in different ways. He also encourages Una Stubbs – a feisty Mrs Pearce – to make her disapproval of Higgins even stronger, which she immediately does with aplomb.

The actors linger over Doolittle's acceptance of the £5 he is offered to go away, Tony finding a way of hinting that there may have to be further payments. There's a brief debate about the morality of the experiment with Eliza, and the two men's attitude to it. "It's a kind of Faustian deal, taking someone and changing them," Peter says. "That's what the play is about." Eliza then appears, fresh from her much-needed bath. Michelle Dockery, a real cockney East Ender and proud of it, makes an impressively authentic flower-girl. Her Eliza is vigorous yet vulnerable, her coarse vowels not yet tamed by Higgins' efforts. Peter asks for a different emphasis on one line, pointing out: "She's a *good* girl, as opposed to the bad ones in Tottenham Court Road."

The action then shifts to Act 3, and Mrs Higgins's flat in Chelsea. Barbara Jefford plays the initial scene with Tim with assurance and authority, vainly trying to curb her son's bad manners as he gatecrashes her At Home event. It flows well, with little need for any notes from Peter. But the delightful scene which follows, marking Eliza's first outing into society, is more complex, with seven characters on stage, and a network of relationships needing to be established.

Michelle's voice is now startlingly transformed, from a rasping to a mellifluous tone. As Eliza holds court, she subtly conveys the studied formality of her absurd pronouncements. After she delivers the famous exit line "I am going in a taxi" that so shocked the play's first audience, Peter suggests an alternative way of playing it. This time she says the last word more wistfully. "'Now she's in love with taxis," he remarks.

Some time is spent exploring the spiky relationship between Mrs Eynsford Hill and her daughter, a true battle of the generations. Emma Noakes is a saucy, provocative Clara, openly flirting with Higgins, while Pamela Miles is movingly distraught as her mother. Peter suggests she could be even more anguished. "This is a family row in someone else's house," he points out. "It's an explosive situation." She plays the moment again, effectively taking the agony up a notch.

The atmosphere throughout the rehearsal is happily collaborative. Peter welcomes ideas from the actors, and they respond readily to his many suggestions. Mostly he delivers his thoughts from behind his desk, with associate director Cordelia Monsey chipping in now and then with ideas. But sometimes he moves into the playing area, to talk in more detail and depth with one or two of the actors.

His method is to keep an extremely close watch on the script, and to ensure that the actors suit the thought to the word, the word to the thought, conveying exactly the meaning Shaw intended, down to the last syllable. There is an amusing moment when he questions James' emphasis on the first syllable of "sanguinary", Pickering's euphemism for "bloody". James says promptly: "I've looked it up," as indeed his character would have done. He gets his way.

The last hour is spent rehearsing the beginning of Act 4. Higgins, Pickering and Eliza have returned from the garden party and the opera, the two men slightly drunk. The essence of the scene is their disregard for Eliza now that she has been successfully passed off as a duchess and the experiment is over. "Their renunciation of the scheme is terrible for Eliza to hear," Peter suggests.

Here, as earlier, Tim and James establish an excellent rapport. The question arises, Do they actually see Eliza in the room? It's agreed that they do, which makes their behaviour even more harsh. They play the scene with suitable callousness, while Michelle silently conveys Eliza's shattered emotions through her expression and body language. During a pause she observes: "I have an image of me sitting between them in a cab for the last half-hour, and being completely ignored."

"What the devil have I done with my slippers?" Higgins asks, and there the morning session ends. Peter appears very satisfied with progress. "It's terrifically difficult, but it's coming along well," he tells the actors. "It's very rich." As they break for lunch Tim remarks: "I always thought *Pygmalion* was a good play, but now I think it's a great one."

2

Shakespeare

Richard II – Henry V – Twelfth Night – The Tempest

Stripping Away the History

At the end of a full day's rehearsal at the Old Vic, Trevor Nunn and his creative team explained to me their attempt to create a totally new staging of Richard II.

SOME DIRECTORS BEGIN REHEARSALS WITH a read-through of the play. Others start by blocking the action. Trevor Nunn does neither of these, at least not with Shakespeare. "I believe it's impossible for an ad hoc group of actors with many different kinds of experience to start rehearsing a Shakespeare play without a full introduction to his world and his heightened language," he says.

So when his company assembled to start work on

Richard II, he spent the first two days working with them on Shakespeare's text, and in particular the verse. For the rest of the week he embarked on a detailed investigation of the play. "We looked at what it means both on and below the surface, at its imagery and progression, and at the extraordinary character insights Shakespeare has, which perhaps aren't apparent on the first reading. It's very important that all options are discussed, and we establish a coherent approach."

We're talking at the end of a full day of rehearsals, which he is conducting in an airy, spacious rehearsal room at the top of the Old Vic, inhabited by many a ghost of Richards past, including John Gielgud and Alec Guinness. Surprisingly, though he has directed thirty of Shakespeare's thirty-seven plays, Nunn has never tackled *Richard II*. The idea of doing so emerged out of conversations he and Kevin Spacey had over the last two years, during which they discussed several possible Shakespeare roles for Spacey to take on.

"For Richard you need an actor who is capable of flamboyant role-playing, and expressing every kind of mood and indulgence," Nunn argues. "But he also has to be interested in a character's interior life, because by the end of the play that's all that Richard is left with. Kevin has shown that he can deliver fantastic pizzazz, but his greatest strength lies in his ability to strip away a character's layers, to show what's really going on underneath. Despite his film stardom he's a genuine stage actor, and his skill in rehearsal is there for all to see."

One of the first decisions Nunn had to make was whether to approach *Richard II* as a medieval history play, or to try to find in it a contemporary relevance. Shakespeare's plays invariably have different meanings for different generations or cultures, depending on the issues current in a particular society. *Henry V*, for instance, has been viewed at one time as a hymn to patriotism, at another as an anti-war play. *Richard II*, Nunn believes, can similarly be interpreted in different ways.

"The play asks a large number of vital questions about our country, our history, our traditions and institutions. It was politically dangerous when Shakespeare wrote it because, as far as Queen Elizabeth was concerned, everything about the succession was speculative and unresolved. People were asking questions about the future of the monarchy, and what would happen if rebellion took place in the country. After Elizabeth's death the play went unperformed for a very long time. But it came back into favour in the twentieth century; during the 1936 abdication crisis, for example, it seemed to have a disturbing relevance."

So what does he think its particular resonance is today? "We live in a questioning age, at a time when everything about our institutions is being seriously challenged. There's the issue of the monarchy and the republican debate. There are arguments about our parliamentary system: is it any longer valid, or just a kind of circus, a medieval showcase? People also question our fancy-dress legal system, and whether trial by jury is viable. These are all issues which lend Shakespeare's plays an unexpected relevance."

Given these thoughts, it's perhaps unsurprising that Nunn opted to strip away traditional associations and go for a more contemporary production, with the aim not just of laying bare the essence of the play, but also connecting it to our current concerns about surveillance, the abuse of power, and political integrity. Here a fluid setting and the use of state-of-the-art technology has been crucial, the results of his working closely with his designer and a team of video-design experts.

Hildegard Bechtler designed his 1999 production of *The Merchant of Venice* at the National, and their collaboration on *Richard II* has followed a similar pattern, as she explains: "Once Trevor had talked to me about his ideas, I began to collect a whole range of references, from newspapers, magazines, art galleries, and photographers. I concentrated on those that showed public spaces, in parliament and the corridors of power, spaces with plush carpets and panelling, spaces that had no intimacy. I also gathered images of people: of royalty, of the aristocracy in their stately homes, of politicians both in public and private."

These images were then fed back to Nunn, and helped to move his ideas on further. "I was energised by the way Hildegard picked up on those aspects of our age that retain a medievalism or Gothicism, or something heraldic or traditional. A great deal of panoply still exists, and a great deal of dressing-up – in this country we seem to need that reassurance that nothing has changed. So the design has incorporated many of these elements."

Another crucial element has been the decision to use screens on which to project various kinds of images. Nunn explains: "There is a large-scale, epic dimension to the events in *Richard II*, which we can hint at and make part of the production's world through the use of recorded images. Film also enables us to underline Shakespeare's exploration of the disparity between how people behave in private and how they behave for public consumption. And the matter of how you project yourself as a leader, that has so much to do with mass communication."

This was where the video-design team from Mesmer – who worked with Nunn on *The Woman in White* and Tom

Stoppard's *The Coast of Utopia* – came into the equation. Meeting with the director, and working from an annotated script in which he indicated where he wanted images to be used, Dick Straker and Sven Ortel responded with ideas about the most appropriate technology to use, and the ways of using it most effectively. As a result some images are captured live and put through a projection system, some are pre-recorded, and some are existing ones used on a large scale.

"Trevor had a road map in his mind, a general plan about the overall structure, but he gave us a lot of freedom over the specifics," Ortel says. "He was interested in the way news is captured and then edited. So we decided to employ the same tools that broadcasters use. This meant that we could manipulate the content, intercut it with archive footage to look as if it is live footage, and edit in other ways."

With the company still in the early stages of rehearsal, many decisions remain to be made – about the amount and content of the screen material, about the clothes to be worn by each actor. Nunn is keen to remain open to ideas during rehearsals, not just from his creative team but also from the actors. "As we stage the play I'm offering ideas, but I'm also receiving them from a group of people who are wonderfully full of invention. It's very much two-way traffic."

This Happy Breed

In the summer of 1994 I watched a group of students in action at a National Theatre event centering on Henry V, *directed by Brigid Lamour.*

IT'S THE NIGHT BEFORE AGINCOURT. The tension is getting to the English soldiers. "These are mates of mine, and I know some of them aren't going to make it through the night," one of them shouts at Henry, as the king wanders incognito through the camp.

Conscripted into the English army for the morning, scores of school and college students are scattered around a large rehearsal room at the National, checking armour, cleaning swords, rolling dice, or just musing on what the morrow may bring. The students, aged 14-18, together with their teachers, are taking part in a day devoted to working on *Henry V*. The morning workshop, led by a company of six National actors, is to be followed by a 75-minute version of what is normally a three-hour play.

Under the aegis of the National's education department, the actors have just finished a nine-week tour visiting schools in Shropshire, Wales, Hereford & Worcester, Cambridgeshire and Kent, before returning to London for their final week. They followed the formula used successfully in earlier productions of *Macbeth* and *A Midsummer Night's Dream*, also set up by the education department.

Henry V was chosen because of its powerful themes of national identity, patriotism and war. During the workshop there is a brainstorming session on the causes of war. The students throw up a wealth of ideas that include Greed, Religion, Land, Power, Racism, Ambition, Freedom and Independence. The aim is to show them that a play written several hundred years ago can still raise issues that are fully contemporary. Is Henry justified in waging war against France? What do we feel about his order that all French prisoners be killed? And is the play a call to arms, or one that carries an anti-war message?

The workshop also demonstrates how actors experiment with ideas in rehearsal. As an example, the actors play the opening scene in three different ways: first straight, then as a Commons-style debate, and finally as a furtive conversation in a corridor, with students huddled up close to provide the walls. The contrast is illuminating.

Director Brigid Lamour has chosen to do a promenade performance. "Using this method, we're able to have a very direct relationship between audience and actors," she says. "By moving the audience around, we can have the space populated by more than six actors."

The afternoon shows her decision to have been a good one. The production is stunning in its imaginative use of set, costumes and songs, as well as the high standard of the ensemble work. But the effect is undoubtedly heightened by the audience's physical involvement in the action: the sense of expectation the night before the battle is quite palpable, as are the emotions provoked by Henry's "band of brothers" speech.

Afterwards the students talk animatedly about the play. Here is one group that seems unlikely to forget St Crispin's Day in a hurry.

Illusions in Illyria

In the winter of 2007 I spent a rainy day in Islington with Edward Hall's all-male Propeller company. After touring their production of The Taming of the Shrew *they were tackling* Twelfth Night, *before bringing both plays to the Old Vic.*

THE LIGHTNING FLASHES, THE THUNDER roars, the rain hammers on the skylight. It's an unexpected but appropriate mix of sound effects for the group of actors working inside Finsbury Town Hall, rehearsing a play which begins with a storm and a shipwreck, and ends with the refrain "For the rain it raineth every day".

Director Edward Hall and his all-male Propeller company are three days into rehearsals for Shakespeare's comic, melancholic masterpiece *Twelfth Night*. Previously, in a break from playing *The Taming of the Shrew* in Stratford and other venues, they've spent three weeks examining the text in detail, and brainstorming ideas about how to stage it. Today, in an attractive carpeted room, the size of which matches approximately that of the Old Vic stage, they're putting the play on its feet.

Already working without scripts, they've reached the scene where Feste (Tony Bell) is bantering with Olivia (Dugald Bruce-Lockhart), to the disgust of her self-important steward, Malvolio (Bob Barrett). The challenge here is to find the balance of power between Feste and Malvolio. "You're playing it too phlegmatically," Edward suggests. "There's more at stake than that, the nerve-ends are jangling." He looks for more indignation from Tony, and gets it.

News now comes that Viola has arrived, in male disguise as Caesario, and insists on seeing Olivia to convey her master Orsino's suit. "I think you need to restrain your fury, and find more sarcasm," Edward tells Bob, after Malvolio has angrily described the saucy young fellow at the gates. He does so, making the speech more particular and ambivalent, and therefore more interesting.

There follows a brief but hilarious appearance by a drunken Sir Toby Belch (Jason Baughan), after which a debate takes place about which receptacle he should vomit in. Then Viola (Tam Williams) enters, and confronts the veiled Olivia. Edward wants Tam to make clearer when Viola is articulating her own thoughts ("I am not what I play") and when she is delivering her prepared text. He stresses the frustration of her situation: "All you did was pose as a eunuch in order to serve Orsino, and immediately you fall in love with him, and find yourself having to act as a messenger between him and the woman he claims to love."

They reach the famous Willow Cabin speech, in which Viola describes how she would woo Olivia if she were Orsino. Tam feels he is speaking it too aggressively, and Edward agrees. "You need to keep it lighter, not so earnest. It needs to seem as if you're just making the ideas up on the spot, providing a list of examples of what you would do." The next time around he begins to find the appropriate note. For Dugald, the challenge in the scene is to get the balance right between Olivia's apparent indifference towards Viola, and her actual growing interest. "Should I play it a bit flirty here?" he asks Edward; but when he does so the change seems to come too early.

It's clear that this is no conventional production. There is a kind of chorus in each scene, a handful of actors in white masks scattered around the space who react to the unfolding story. They are, it appears, the spirits of Illyria, inhabiting Olivia's house. Also music is assuming a vital element in the creation of atmosphere. Most of the actors are also musicians, and at different stages are called on to play variously the accordion, guitar, synthesiser, clarinet, xylophone or, more exotically, a Tibetan bowl or a series of pots and pans.

The space is dominated by two enormous wardrobes, semi-transparent on the sides and with mirrors on the front. They have many uses, as exits and entrances and hiding-places, but they also help to create illusion, most notably at moments when Viola needs to be transformed into her identical twin Sebastian, or vice versa.

The fact that the female parts are played by men makes no special impact at this stage. The actors, of course, are thoroughly used to this arrangement. Without the benefit of costume, the cross-gender set-up is only occasionally touched upon, notably in relation to Tam, a man playing a woman disguised as a man.

Edward's style as a director is essentially collaborative. He is skilled at interpreting Shakespeare's text, but often asks the actors for their ideas before suggesting his own. Most of them have worked with him before, some on several Propeller productions, and their conversations about meaning and motivation are markedly relaxed. Energetic yet laid-back, he frequently moves into the acting area, discussing ideas with a variety of gestures as well as words.

After lunch the actors take it from the top, running all the work they have done so far, which is about a quarter of the play. The opening scene in Orsino's court, with the floor strewn with upturned chairs and scattered glasses and bottles, effectively conveys an atmosphere of the morning after the night before, of the revels now being ended. A mournful melody on the violin punctuates Orsino's celebrated "If music be the food of love" speech, which is spoken with convincing passion by Jack Tarlton.

The scene seems in good shape, and needs only minimal attention, as does the brief one that follows, when the shipwrecked Viola first arrives in Illyria. Edward's notes on this chunk of the play concentrate on minor questions of emphasis and pace: he is noticeably rigorous in the pursuit of clarity and, where necessary, speed.

In the day's final session the actors tackle for the first time the start of Act 2, involving Sebastian (Joe Flynn) and his new friend Antonio (Alasdair Craig), who has saved him from drowning. Some time is spent on deciding where precisely the characters are situated. Eventually it's agreed they're in a dark area in the hall of Olivia's house, and that the only lighting will be torchlight.

"It's a scene in which we need to follow Sebastian's emotional undercurrent," Edward says, after the initial run-through. Joe suggests that "He can't deal with being the one twin left alive." Edward agrees: "Yes, he's caught in limbo, and that makes him very bitter." Playing the scene again, Joe conveys effectively Sebastian's anguish over his sister's apparent death. The day ends with a quick rehearsal of one of the moments when the twins effect a quick change via a cupboard. It's a tricky illusion to create, especially in ordinary light, but eventually Joe and Tam get it spot on.

Edward is clearly pleased with progress so far. "The more we work on the play, the more interesting it gets," he tells the actors. "After three days it seems to me to be just dripping with ironic acid."

Roughing out the Magic

In the spring of 2003 director Mark Rosenblatt and designer Jon Bausor explained their thinking about their production of The Tempest, *the latest in the National's "Shakespeare Unplugged" series of schools productions.*

JON BAUSOR IS A SATISFIED man. "The higher up the scale you go in theatre, the more likely it is you will be reading the script on the plane, and having meetings via fax machines,' he says. "With this project we have time and space."

It's late autumn, and for some time now he and director

Mark Rosenblatt have been exploring a plethora of ideas about staging *The Tempest* for young audiences. They began work by reading the text out loud, making sure they knew exactly what every word meant, before deciding whether to go for a promenade, an end-on or traverse staging. "It's hard, very dense language," Mark observes. "With Shakespeare a lot of actors can get to the end of a run and still not know what some of the words mean."

Among the many ideas thrown up in their discussions, two are beginning to firm up. One is to focus on the differing parent-child relationships that abound in the play. Mark suggests, for example, that Miranda, Caliban, Ariel and Ferdinand all want happiness and independence, but have to decide whether to find it themselves or entrust it to their parents.

"Caliban strikes out on his own. Miranda follows her heart when she disobeys Prospero's instructions, and tells Ferdinand her name. Ariel chooses the opposite, and remains obedient in order to get free. Ferdinand has to make his own decisions because he thinks his father is dead. So we're thinking about what parents make children look like in the way they dress."

One idea is to put Ariel initially in a grey-flannel blazer and shorts, as a model child of the 1950s. For Miranda, Jon suggests some kind of Amish-type costume. "Maybe something strict, rigid, almost puritanical, reflecting her upbringing, and the bareness of the schoolroom that is Prospero's cell."

The idea of transformation is basic to this late Shakespeare play, so another theme they've been exploring is that of magic and illusion. But here they've had to keep in mind the fact that their production will be touring to sports halls and schools as well as to conventional theatrical spaces.

"In a hall or gym we can't use the normal devices, such as flying things out or losing them through the trapdoor," Jon says. "We've got to change everything in front of the audience. We thought at first that magical illusion with a cabinet might work in some way, but now we've moved away from that idea as being too tricky, and imposing something on the text."

Between them Mark and Jon have seen four productions of *The Tempest*. "Sometimes I've been bored, and I've asked myself why," Mark says. "I think it's because the play is offered up with this great air of mystery, which affects the tone, so it becomes quite cerebral and funereal. People talk about it being Shakespeare's farewell to the stage, or a metaphor for playwriting, so seeing it in a fresh light becomes quite difficult. But I'm beginning to see points where, for instance, it's much funnier than you at first think."

Other ideas still in the ether relate to sleeping and dreaming, and to the alchemical elements of Baconian science, of the kind that Peter Greenaway overdosed on in his film version of the play, *Prospero's Books*. The pair are also toying semi-seriously with the notion of Big Brother – here, after all, is an omnipotent figure keeping a close watch on a group of people isolated from the rest of society. "But a lot of these ideas won't get through," Jon says."We don't want it to be overly complicated. In the end we're going for simplicity."

3

Modern Plays

The Entertainer – Light Shining in Buckinghamshire –
Speed-the-Plow – National Anthems – No Man's Land –
Resurrection Blues – Under the Fish and Over the Water –
Complicit – Cloaca

1956 and All That

In the spring of 2007 the Old Vic staged a fiftieth-anniversary
production of John Osborne's The Entertainer, *a play which*
has the Suez crisis at its heart. I joined director Sean Holmes,
Robert Lindsay and the rest of the company for their second
week of rehearsals.

STANDING BY THE PIANO IN the corner, Robert Lindsay
launches straight into his song: "Now I'm just an ordinary
bloke/The same as you out there/Not mad for women, I'm

not a soak/I never really care...." He has a rich, resonant voice, but one that can also capture effectively the seediness and the pathos of the fading music-hall entertainer Archie Rice.

On the walls of the large rehearsal room at the top of the Old Vic, beneath a storyboard which shows by means of a series of photographs the play's sequence of scenes, is posted a timeline of the events during the Suez crisis of 1956, that critical moment in British history in which Osborne chose to set his play.

Robert and director Sean Holmes are looking at one of Archie's routines, part monologue, part song. They work out which lines of the song he should sing, and which could be patter. They then go into the acting area to sketch out the moves. "It's a bizarre song," Robert says. "I mustn't forget that he's pissed, and then suddenly has to go on – the actor's nightmare." They discuss the song's content in relation to 1956, its subversive nature reflected in the line "This was their finest *shower*!" Sean observes: "Suez is really a character in the play."

After this musical beginning the day continues with the director and the actors sitting round a table, subjecting two of the key scenes to close analysis. "I'm realising more and more how political the play is," Sean says. He has a copy of the original Samuel French edition, the play as Osborne wrote it, marked with the cuts made for the first production at the Royal Court. During the session he suggests several small cuts, sometimes following the French edition, sometimes not. The actors readily accept his suggestions.

Scene 12 contains two overlapping duologues, so Sean has decided to read and discuss them separately at first, beginning with the imminent split between Archie's daughter Jean (Emma Cunniffe) and her fiancé Graham

(Jim Creighton). After a read-through of the scene, they talk about what might have happened just before. "This is all a discovery for Jean," Emma observes. "She's searching for answers to questions that have arisen in the last few days." Jim chips in: "It's not that Graham is nasty, he's just twenty years out of date." A second reading helps to illuminate these thoughts.

Next up for discussion is the scene of the Rice family's return home from the funeral of Archie and Phoebe's son Mick. "There's a variety of levels of drunkenness and grief here," Sean suggests. "Everyone's going on about the past, while Jean thinks they ought all to be tub-thumping and facing reality." They read the scene, then identify certain problems. Pam Ferris (Phoebe) wonders about her line describing Archie, "He's always been good to me," observing: "It seems a strange way to defend him, given his behaviour. You wonder what her standards are." Sean agrees. "She can be quite contradictory about his women. But I think those contradictions give her character."

A query about Archie's line "scarper the letty" prompts an answer from John Normington, playing Archie's father Billy. He believes it's a phrase of Polari, the gay slang used at the time, and means "flee the lodgings". When they reach Jean's line, "What's it all in aid of – is it really just for the sake of a gloved hand waving at you from a golden coach?" Sean recalls that Laurence Olivier, the original Archie Rice, disliked such anti-monarch sentiments, and succeeded in getting the line cut when the original Royal Court production transferred to the West End.

During a short break Robert casually picks up a stick, puts on his hat, and starts to rehearse a couple of tap-dance routines. He's an extremely nifty hoofer, with an easy, relaxed style. Good enough surely, as with his voice, to be able to sing and dance in the third-rate manner required by Archie Rice.

It's time to move back to scene 12, containing the duologue between Archie and Brother Bill (Andrew McDonald) about the choice facing Archie, either to emigrate to Canada or go to jail. The accepted view is that Archie means what he says when he rejects Bill's offer of Canada. But Robert throws in a different thought: "My impression when I first read the play was that he does go to Canada. Maybe that's why Phoebe comes to get him right at the end? Of course it could be played both ways, but I need to know which." They agree to explore this idea further.

At the end of the session Sean observes: "I think the play is more relevant now than it was even ten years ago, given all the current discussions about Britishness and identity. And you know that we'll eventually pull out of Iraq, and people will ask, What did they die for, just as this family does in relation to Mick's death."

After lunch the actors are on their feet, translating the morning's ideas into practice. Bubbling over with ideas, Sean frequently springs up from his seat, stopping the action when a fresh one comes to mind, and talking it through with the actors, who clearly respect his judgement and find his approach to the play stimulating.

They focus on the post-funeral scene where, as Sean puts it, "it's like they've all been lobotomised". Pam eloquently conveys Phoebe's sadness in her silence and stillness, while Robert and John are effectively irritating as they deliberately reminiscence about the price of draught cider at this tragic moment. Emma meanwhile convincingly brings out Jean's anger and frustration at Archie ("You're a bastard on wheels!").

The tension in the scene, Sean suggests, is about when

the revelation will come that Archie intends to divorce Phoebe. Meanwhile he considers restoring some lines of Billy's which he had cut in the morning. "They make us realise that he used to have a home, and now all he has is a decanter in the pawn shop, and a ticket for it. I think they're rather wonderful, so let's put them back in."

John delivers Billy's speech about the good old days of the music hall with a touching grace. Sean points out that it makes clear to Archie that his father never rated him as a performer. Robert suggests Billy might give a little hint of his old act, and John responds with some tentative movements. Sean likes the idea, and thinks they might shift this section to in front of the proscenium arch. "It's an incredibly rich scene," Pam observes. Robert adds: "With a very mucky undercurrent."

By the end of the day it's clearly juicing nicely. "I really didn't understand it until we started working on it," Sean admits. As the actors begin to leave, he adds: "It's a brilliant, state-of-the nation play, but also very like Strindberg in the way the family pulls itself apart. I think it's a classic."

A Different Resonance

The National's mobile touring production of Caryl Churchill's play Light Shining in Buckinghamshire *played in a wide variety of venues during the winter of 1996-97. I caught up with it in a church in Brighton, and talked to her briefly after the performance.*

CARYL CHURCHILL LOOKS QUIZZICALLY ROUND the vast cavernous church. "This is the first time I've had any worries about the blasphemous parts of the script," she confesses.

You could see her point. She and the rest of us in the audience at St Martin's Church in Brighton had just witnessed a powerful performance of her 1976 play *Light Shining in Buckinghamshire*, in which descriptions of Christ as "a bastard", Mary as "no virgin", and God as "a great bully" had been ringing round the altar and choir stalls where the piece was being performed.

The play is in fact a deeply moral piece, exploring with great passion the revolutionary beliefs that broke out during the English civil war. It looks in particular at the subversive notions of the Diggers and the Levellers, and the Ranters' millennium belief that Christ would soon come to establish heaven on earth.

This latest mobile production by the National is the first professional staging of the play since the Royal Court version twenty years ago. Its subject matter seems suddenly topical. "It does have a rather different resonance now," Caryl Churchill agrees. "Especially when you bear in mind the millennium, the land-protest movement, and the Labour Party moving to the right." Director Mark Wing-Davey also sees parallels. During rehearsals he went with the cast to the now-demolished eco-village in Wandsworth. "It was very like the Digger community established by Winstanley on common land in Weybridge. It fell apart because people came in who didn't share the original ideals."

The programme for *Light Shining in Buckinghamshire* provides valuable background information on the period and the various revolutionary ideas then current. It also includes a selection of contemporary writings selected by Tony Benn, who came to talk to the actors about the Levellers and their later influence.

The play, challenging but rewarding, is the sixth of Caryl

Churchill's works that Mark Wing-Davey has directed. "I love the way she plays with form and structure," he says. "I also find it fascinating that the play has in it so many seeds of her latest obsessions." In the famous Putney Debates, which form a central part of the play, he's tried to avoid caricature – for example, of the bourgeois General Ireton. "The temptation is to play him as a Machiavellian character, when in fact he's committed to discussion as much as anyone else."

The debates are played in a straightforward manner, allowing the arguments to breathe for themselves. Stylistically the production is full of invention, with costumes and props from all periods, and characters played by more than one actor – a device suggested by Caryl Churchill, who explains: "Doing this seems to reflect better the reality of large events such as war and revolution, where many people share the same kind of experience."

Digging Below the Surface

During rehearsals in the spring of 2008 of David Mamet's Speed-the-Plow *at the Old Vic, its director Matthew Warchus and its stars Kevin Spacey, Jeff Goldblum and Laura Michelle Kelly shared with me their ideas about working on the play.*

JC Can I first ask you, Kevin, in your role as artistic director of the theatre, what made you choose to stage *Speed-the-Plow*?

Kevin Spacey When I'm choosing a play it's not just in isolation. I try to appeal to slightly different audiences with each production. I thought this was a great way to balance the season. We've had *All About My Mother*, a new and challenging work, and the panto *Cinderella*, which is a uniquely British occasion, and we follow the Mamet with Shaw's *Pygmalion*. I've always liked *Speed-the-Plow*. It's a great actors' work by a great American writer, and it's very funny, dynamic and entertaining. Like a lot of Mamet's work, its language is what interests me. That's what I find most challenging as we stumble our way through these first days of rehearsal.

JC And what made you decide to direct the play, Matthew?

Matthew Warchus I've always had a great feeling for it, because it's like a modern, sharp, edgy, aggressive, funny parable. It's got a huge dimension which is belied by its taut, tiny, minuscule scale. It's like splitting an atom and finding stuff inside: it's got the biggest themes and profound ideas. And yet it lives in a very slick, contemporary, jazzy, tight, clenched-fist world. It's not romantic or epic, but it covers massive themes and ideas.

The theme of art and commerce is one with which we all are confronted every day. It's very immediate to us. It's a play that touches on values, how to live your life, how we have lost values and principles and real connections, how we all live through this noisy, corrupt, vulgar, cheapened version of life. It's like a poem, and the language works like that as well. It's like a very profound poem. It's very funny as well, so it delivers this punch inside a comedy form.

JC And Jeff, is the Hollywood that Mamet shows us one that you recognise?

Jeff Goldblum A lot of it is familiar. I know Los Angeles and the things they're talking about, places, houses, the kind of homes where the middle act takes place. I'm an actor in Hollywood, so I stay out of the business side as much as possible. I'm glad to have my trusty representatives, so I stay as little focussed as possible on the business side. I don't subscribe to the trade papers, I don't get a thrill out of seeing who the names and changing faces and the big shots are at the studio. But I brush against all that, so I avoid eating in places where such people might go.

What the place is for business people in making a movie and producing lovely stories in one form or other, and what their relationship might be with the people who actually make them, how they can contribute, I'm familiar with that territory and those issues. These offices, I've been there, I know the kind of talk and I know these kinds of people that Mamet makes use of in that poetic way. We're doing it in the original 1980s period, and I was there at that time.

JC So what attracted you to the play, Laura?

Laura Michelle Kelly I like the questions it raises about why movies should be made, and the idea of audiences suddenly having an insight into what happens behind the scenes of the films they see. I like the moral issues, such as which films to champion at the business level. It's got me thinking. It's a very rhythmic play, and it's nice to see all the changes of pace. I like that. It's a unique style, which I'm learning from scratch.

KS We've been talking in rehearsal about Mamet's language. In many ways it feels like you're learning another language, but there's also something very familiar about the way the characters speak. We've been investigating not only what is said, but the double meanings, then the things that are hidden below, then things that are driven below that, then agendas, personalities, relationships, friendships. So it's quite complex.

For me part of the joy of working on it has been not just in trying to learn the lines and get the rhythms right, so that it isn't just about pattern, or two or three actors playing ping-pong with each other. What has been great in terms of what Matthew has been helping us carve out is how to make sure within those rhythms and that pace that we really listen to each other, so there's a real sense that you hear what is being said. In many ways the play is about how people hear things, and how therefore they interpret them, and how that leads to another decision or another comment. On the surface it's very funny and it moves like a bat out of hell, but it's the subterranean stuff that we've been exploring and playing with.

MW The language that Bobby and Charlie use is a language which Karen doesn't understand or speak, which is not surprising, because it's a challenge for *us* to decide whether they're serious or not. They've got their own sort of code and habit of speaking in an artificial way without communicating on a profound level, so they're using that as a shield. Karen is at odds with that; she has her own language in the middle act, which is dominated by her language, which is something that Bobby doesn't understand.

So there's a collision of language, as well as a collision of love and fear. Fear is present in Bobby and Charlie's words, as well as the paranoia of competition, and survival, and then there's the love and compassion and openness and imaginative flight of Karen. It's a tragedy in that fear and love collide, and fear wins in the end, when you hope love will. Each of the three characters is on the throne for one act, first Bobby and then Karen and then Charlie, who seizes power and wreaks destruction.

KS The play *National Anthems*, which we did last year, also had three characters. There's something about the dynamic of that, especially when one of them is a stranger, which Karen is. It's really interesting what happens in a marriage or a relationship or a friendship when a stranger enters. You don't know what's going to happen when those people collide. And how easily it can go from two people fighting for someone's attention to two against one, all those shifts that happen within that kind of dynamic.

MW Three characters also means it will automatically be competitive, they're competing to be number one, so that dynamic is changing. Mamet alludes to that when he has Charlie say to Karen, "Because I love this guy too." He's making quite an obvious play of that, of those allegiances, of the power struggle.

JC Thinking about Mamet's rapid-fire language, are you approaching the text in a different way from how you might work on, say, a Miller or O'Neill play?

MW Working on the language in rehearsal, it feels close to Beckett, in that you're often asking, "Is there a pause there?" It's that kind of rigour. It certainly means you have to learn the lines very early, because it's quite difficult to play incomplete lines in an approximate way. You're dependent on being interrupted quite fast.

KS And sometimes there's the question, "Is that an interruption, or is it that the character doesn't know the word to say next, so do they stop themselves?" At the end of the day it's a matter for interpretation, even though Mamet makes very clear indications where beats happen. There is this discovery of "Do you think it's that or is it this?", "Do I mean that?", "Do I know what I'm going to say here?" It's so important for us to know what those thoughts are, what the complete thought is, even if you don't get a chance to express it, or it gets cut off, or it suddenly takes a left turn and goes somewhere else that you didn't expect, and you forget it for four pages, and then you bring it up again. If you're just looking at the text it feels like interrupted thoughts, but in fact there's a through line happening with all these characters.

JG It's quite a delicious little challenge to go, "How exactly is this intricate trio or duet going to be played?" So you find the rhythm. A lot of it is laid out by Mamet, but you have to invent a lot too, find a lot, and justify why it goes like that.

LMK The fighting between the fear and the love is a really strong thing, and how that would affect these two grotesque characters in the beginning with all their disgusting language and the fiercely violent kind of things that happen in Act 3, and how Karen would affect that scene, is interesting to work out, though I haven't found the answers yet.

KS I would say that even though this play is about an industry, if you think about the last twenty-five years and all these behind-the-scenes documentaries, and special items on DVDs, a large amount of the public knows much more about the movie business than they did thirty or forty years ago. There's a familiarity. But ultimately it's not about just this particular industry. You can take these kinds of characters and put them at the head of a shipping line or an oil company. The morality questions such as, "Do you do something just for money or for some greater ideal or a greater good?" are ones that any business faces.

We see the result of what the movie industry's choices are, and while it's true that an enormous amount of complaints and criticisms are made about the movie business, we also have to say that there is an endless amount of incredible great films that are inspiring, that we love to this day. It's about those people who have straddled that line: you go back to the Irving Thalbergs of the movie world, they somehow had one foot in the business world and one foot in the artistic camp.

MW It's interesting, because Mamet has such an aggressive, cynical signature, but he's clearly a very romantic idealist, because the argument is about something that can actually change things. He's still in the thick of it, working in LA, but still believing in quite pure things as a writer.

Painting in the Detail

In the spring of 2005 I watched Kevin Spacey and his co-stars Mary Stuart Masterson and Steven Weber getting to grips together with director David Grindley with another three-character play, Dennis McIntyre's intense domestic drama National Anthems.

IT'S THE PLACE WHERE PRACTICALLY all the great names of the British theatre profession have worked over the last ninety years. But today the spacious, high-ceilinged room at the top of the Old Vic echoes to the unfamiliar sound of American voices, as the cast of *National Anthems* get to grips with the story, which concerns a couple living in Michigan whose party is gate-crashed by an unsettling stranger, and the effect it has on their lives.

It's only the fifth day of rehearsal for Kevin Spacey and his two co-stars. But for certain sections of the first act of Dennis McIntyre's hard-hitting play they are already virtually off the book. Under the observant eye of director David Grindley they're starting to explore the tensions and undercurrents that lie beneath the taut, tense, often humorous dialogue of the first act. The three actors have clearly already established an excellent rapport: the work is serious and intensive, the atmosphere jokey and informal.

Before today they had spent three days "researching" their characters in detail. David had interviewed each of them individually, encouraging them to create their character's biography. He had then brought Steven Weber and Mary Stuart Masterson together, so they could iron out any differences in their stories, and present a consistent, shared biography of the couple, Arthur and Lesley Reed. The next step was to ask them to improvise key moments or issues in their back story: when they met, what arguments they usually have, what happened at the party earlier in the evening, and much more. Finally all three actors had come together to improvise their first meeting.

Today Stephen is wearing a suit ("I'm dressed as Arthur"), while Kevin and Mary Stuart are more casually dressed. The trio are working within a minimal set: there are two well-used sofas and a low table centre stage, a newly made and painted door-frame to one side, and a couple of boxes down stage which stand in for the Reeds' trendy Bang & Olufsen speakers. The actors have seen the set model, but for the moment the rest of the house and the expensive, status-defining furnishings and fittings have to be imagined.

This is only the second day the actors have been on their feet. As they begin to work through the opening section they stop now and then, to try to pin down the detail of their characters' motivation. Steven and Mary Stuart ponder on how the Reeds handle their first meeting with the stranger Ben Cook, played by Kevin.

David's basic method as director is to offer comments and suggestions and raise questions, but also to ask the actors for their thoughts and feelings. "Everything is up for grabs," he tells them. They respond readily to this invitation, constantly coming up with ideas about their characters' changes in mood or thought, or suggesting alternative moves. David reminds them about what he calls "nesting" – the odd words they add to the text at the beginning or end of a speech, simply because they're not yet secure on their lines. "The writing is very precise, and it needs to be exact," he emphasises. "But we can pick up on that at a later stage." One particular line then prompts a general discussion – lasting a good twenty minutes – about the pressure in American society to succeed in work.

The exchanges during the morning between director and actors have been open, intelligent, questioning and focused. During the lunch break David talks appreciatively about the actors. "Kevin is as fearless as they come. He brings great enthusiasm and energy to the play. He has a lot of status in this room, but he doesn't play on that at all. All he's concerned about is the show, and wanting to make it succeed. With Steven and Mary Stuart, the key thing is that they want to be here: they are both very bright and committed, and extremely enthusiastic, so they're grabbing the reins and riding away."

One of his concerns has been to ensure that, as a British director working with Americans on a play set in America, he knows what he's talking about. "That's why the research on my trip to Detroit with the designer Jonathan Fensom was so important. Having visited that world, I now have a better understanding of the references in the play." To help everyone else, he's displayed on the walls of the rehearsal room an extensive collection of Jonathan's pictures of Detroit, together with maps and background information on the city, and a range of typical American images and ads from the period.

During the afternoon session, photographer Andy Lane is moving discreetly around the room taking pictures. The actors seem completely unfazed by his presence: all three of course are quite used to the cameras from their film and television work.

It's noticeable as the time goes on how willing and quick all three of them are to experiment with different ways of playing the same scene or speech, without any prompting from David. By the end of a creative and fruitful day, in which they have already started to paint in the detail of their characters, David is clearly delighted with progress. "It's been very good," he tells the actors. "It's early days yet of course, but this stuff is really firing."

Pinter Revisited

In 2001 the National revived Harold Pinter's much-discussed play No Man's Land. *Looking back at the original production, I wondered how the successors to John Gielgud and Ralph Richardson would be able to match those legendary performances, and deal with being directed by the playwright himself.*

ONE OF THE FIRST PLAYS to be put on in the new building on the South Bank, *No Man's Land* opened in the Lyttelton in April 1976, after a run in the Old Vic, the National's "temporary home" since 1963. So it seems appropriate that, twenty-five years on, Pinter's powerfully enigmatic play should return to the same theatre at the National.

Back then the director was Peter Hall; this time it's to be Pinter himself. The earlier production was notable for the superb performances of John Gielgud and Ralph Richardson, playing respectively the seedy, garrulous poet Spooner, and the wealthy, patrician man-of-letters Hirst, whose Hampstead house Spooner invades. In November, for the play's return to the Lyttelton, those parts are to be played by two other fine actors, John Wood and Corin Redgrave.

Over the last quarter of a century *No Man's Land* has been analysed to death. On first reading it Hall decided it was about opposites: "Genius against lack of talent, success against failure, drink against sobriety, elegance against uncouthness, smoothness against roughness, politeness against violence."

Gielgud liked the play straightaway, having long been an admirer of Pinter's work. It was he who insisted that the script be sent to Richardson, whom Hall and Pinter feared might not be up to learning the part. But Richardson was equally enthusiastic, despite a later moment of alarm when he feared the play might be "entirely about queers".

In rehearsal the two theatrical knights – Hall called them the Old Lions – struggled to adapt to Pinter's writing method. "There was terror in the rehearsal room when we reached a pause, because each of them thought the other had lost his lines," Hall remembered. In frustration Richardson asked Pinter how many pauses made a silence. "About three, sometimes four, depending on the speech," the playwright helpfully replied. Later Pinter admitted: "I did occasionally offer an emphasis that seemed to be appropriate and called for."

Basing his character partly on the poet W. H. Auden, Gielgud astonished everyone by showing an unexpected talent for impersonation. But Richardson also gave an outstanding and moving performance. The production was a huge commercial success for the National, transferring to the West End and then to Broadway.

Pinter of course is a theatrical jack-of-all-trades. When the play was revived at the Almeida in 1992, with Paul

Eddington as Spooner, he took on the role of Hirst. In rehearsal he told director David Leveaux: "You must be yourself in this situation. You will direct and I will be the actor." Now that he's stepping into the director's shoes, what will he be saying to the National's new Hirst and Spooner?

Resurrecting Late Miller

In the spring of 2006 veteran Hollywood legend Robert Altman came to the Old Vic to direct Arthur Miller's Resurrection Blues. *During rehearsals I watched him working with a starry cast that included Maximilian Schell, James Fox, Neve Campbell and Matthew Modine, and listened to his thoughts about directing Miller's late play.*

A Filmic Eye

DUTHY HALL IN SOUTHWARK, a short walk from the Old Vic. It's the end of the second week of rehearsals for *Resurrection Blues*. A full-scale, multi-level set fills the spacious room. Seated at desks facing the set are members of the creative team and the stage management. Behind them, on a high chair against the back wall, beret on head, sits Robert Altman.

During the course of the day he moves ever closer to the set, as he engages with the developing story. At lunchtime he's shifted down to a sofa in front of the desks; by the end of the day he's up on his feet, moving onto the set to make points to the company about Miller's script. The atmosphere throughout is laid-back but purposeful: Altman clearly trusts his actors, and the feeling is mutual.

They begin from the top, literally. Perched precariously on the edge of the highest platform, which doubles as a mountain top, Neve Campbell is sitting in a wheelchair. She runs through Jeanine's long prologue speech a couple of times, establishing with Altman how paralysed she is supposed to be. "Use your arm more," he tells her. "It's your only means of expression, so don't be afraid to overdo it for now. Be more graphic." She becomes so, and the speech, which she already has by heart, is more effective as a result.

Next up is a scene between Felix (Maximilian Schell), a General, and Stanley (Peter McDonald), a disciple of the mysterious, saintly revolutionary whose actions propel the story, and whom Felix has just had arrested. Max – as everyone calls the celebrated Swiss actor – has his script to hand, but with his resonant voice he is already emanating power and authority, while Peter subtly suggests the dreamy, spaced-out quality of his hippie character.

Altman, in neat fawn shirt and dark trousers, rarely intervenes, usually to comment on tempo and rhythm as much as on character. "Don't make a three-act play of it," he tells Peter on one line, and on another, "Break it up more." His filmic eye attuned to the smallest visual detail, he is concerned about the movements of the three guards. "You should flow in and out of the light, so I know you're there, but I don't really see you," he explains.

At this moment he raises a question about the actors' positions on the set. Designer Robin Wagner brings over the black-box set model he has constructed, and sets it down beside Altman, together with a bunch of tiny figures representing the actors. Altman now has his toy, and the opportunity to test his ideas manually. After a brief discussion between designer and director, the question is resolved.

When the actors resume, Max, an experienced director himself, offers the occasional suggestion. "Should I use the gun more?" "Suppose I sit here?" Altman is happy with his ideas. Their mutually respectful relationship, frequently laced with humour, is also on show in the scene they rehearse next, one in which Felix woos the film director Emily (Jane Adams) over dinner. At the start Max spontaneously tosses a couple of lobster legs over his shoulder. "You're throwing them at one of my actors," Altman says. "He's only a guard," comes Max's reply.

It's an overtly sexual scene, which the actors tackle with relish and humour. Jane is quick to absorb ideas, keen to experiment, using her mobile face and angular body to good effect as Emily realises the strength of her bargaining position. Max manages to make Felix's confused emotions at once ridiculous and sympathetic, as his passion for her overwhelms his political judgement.

After they've run the scene through once, Max says: "At first I think he just uses little looks, although he is very horny." "Yes," Altman replies, "but at my age I can't use that word." They spend a while deciding how far Emily should be responding to Felix's advances. Jane speculatively rests her leg on Max's thigh, then asks: "Should it go higher?" Altman: "No, you shouldn't be too sexually aggressive." Jane: "But I'm about to talk about his willy." Altman: "You don't have to touch it to talk about it."

The scene is a tricky one physically, as the actors have to juggle with their scripts as well as with pieces of lobster, wine, wine glasses, and a bottle. Wine is spilt, scripts tumble onto their plates of food; but once these problems are sorted out the scene begins to flow. After they've run it for the fourth time Altman observes: "Good, many new things came through that time."

During a break there's a discussion about how to use the next day, which is a Saturday. Assistant director Jeremy Whelehan suggests they set up line rehearsals, with understudies hearing the lines of the actors they are covering. Altman says he may or may not join them: "It seems to me you guys made more progress yesterday when I wasn't here," he says. Max observes: "Sometimes it's good to go with your own rhythm. But on Monday you'll come in full of new ideas." Altman replies mildly: "At this stage I think the old ideas will do."

The final session is devoted to the second scene, a long, complicated one involving Emily, Felix, Skip the television executive (Matthew Modine), Felix's cousin Henri Schulz (James Fox), a cameraman, a soundwoman, the police captain, and members of the ensemble. "Use as many props as you can," Altman says, as ponchos and sombreros are donned by the ensemble. "I'm not going to interrupt." He's nearly as good as his word, and the actors work their way through the complexities of the scene. Matthew is already comfortably in the skin of his cynical media man. James, looking suitably academic as Henri, has a more difficult task, being almost entirely an observer of the scene, his substantial dialogue being in other ones.

Eventually the scene becomes muddled, and the actors stumble over their lines. Altman stands up for the first time. "We can't stage this properly until you have the tempo," he says. "If one person forgets a line and breaks the rhythm, it throws the others." Again he picks up on small details: "Someone needs to show the guards how to stand, and how to handle their guns," he suggests.

Jane wants to go back over a few moments, but he denies her the chance: he's not yet prepared to delve in any detail into character motivation. Then comes a piece of pure Altman: "We don't have to hear every word – it's okay if it's a bit of a mish-mash. I don't care what you're saying to your mother on the phone, Jane. People don't have to hear every line."

With that he turns towards the door. "Thank you, and good night." The company applaud.

Altman: Fifty Years of Theatre

Famous worldwide for his quirky, iconoclastic work for the cinema, the creator of acclaimed films such as *Gosford Park*, *Short Cuts*, *The Player* and *Nashville* has also directed plays on and off Broadway, and staged and co-written operas in Chicago. The medium, he says, makes little difference to his way of working.

"You're dealing with the same elements really: the actors have to do the work, and you just watch. At the moment I'm looking at *Resurrection Blues* visually and rhythmically. The psychological content is mostly there: Arthur Miller provided that, and the actors get it, so I don't have to help much."

Laconic and humorous, his mind razor-sharp and his pale-blue eyes alert, he's talking during a break in rehearsals. This modest explanation of his role is of course less than the full story, as Jeremy Whelehan confirms. "Bob makes it seems so effortless, and yet just by virtue of his presence he allows something greater than the sum of its parts to take place. When he gives a piece of direction it's very, very smart."

Altman's career in theatre began half a century ago, when he worked briefly at the Resident Theatre in Kansas City, his home town. In 1981, at the start of a dip in his

Hollywood fortunes, he directed *Rattlesnake in a Cooler* and *Precious Blood*, two plays by Frank South, in Los Angeles and Off-Broadway. He then moved to Broadway to stage *Come Back to the Five and Dime, Jimmy Dean, Jimmy Dean*, starring Cher, Sandy Dennis and Karen Black; he also filmed the play, as well as Sam Shephard's *Fool for Love* and, for television, Pinter's *The Dumb Waiter* and *The Room*.

His involvement in opera has also been significant. After staging Stravinsky's *The Rake's Progress* in Michigan and Lille, he directed and co-wrote *McTeague* with composer William Bolcom for the Lyric Opera of Chicago. In 2004 he returned there to direct *A Wedding*, an opera based on his own 1978 film, which he co-wrote with Arnold Weinstein, with Bolcom again providing the music. A master at working with large casts, Altman reduced the number of characters from forty-eight to sixteen. His freewheeling, sell-out production was widely praised.

While clearly valuing this operatic experience, he finds he has more room for manoeuvre and invention when working on a play. "The tempo is set in opera, they all start and end at the same time. I can't stretch or shrink these things, I have to put everything in to fit the music. With a play, I can make my own tempo."

An acquaintance rather than a friend of Miller ("We had some time and dinners together"), he never discussed *Resurrection Blues* with the playwright, although Miller knew shortly before he died that Altman was going to direct the play at the Old Vic. Its appeal, he says, was partly just because it was by Miller, but also because "there's a different humour level in it than in his other plays; it's more of a reach for him."

He was attracted by the fact that it was a new work. An

early draft of the play was first performed at the Guthrie Theatre, Minneapolis in 2002, but Miller continued to work on it, substantially developing it and completing the new version just before he died in February 2005. It will be having its premiere at the Old Vic.

After two weeks of working on the text with the company, Altman has encountered many surprises. "I'd only read it once when I agreed to do it, and at my age and with my state of mind I don't retain things so well. So now as I watch it unfold it's all very fresh to me. It's even better than I thought it was – but then I'm very bad at reading scripts. I have to see the people and hear the voices."

Set designer Robin Wagner, who also worked with him on *A Wedding* in Chicago, implicitly denies this last point. "Bob and I have collaborated from the very beginning. I showed him pictures of the Andes, and he loved the idea of a set in the mountains, where there would be places to climb, and parts of the scenes would appear and disappear in the mist. As soon as I showed him the model he began to see all kinds of possibilities, and wanted to stage them. He's extremely imaginative and spontaneous, always looking for something that's not written."

Jenny Beavan, who's designing the costumes, praises Altman's openness and flexibility. "Initially he was clear what he wanted some of the characters to look like, and not so clear about others," she explains. "He wanted a timeless feel, and stressed the importance of colour. Now, when I try out ideas on him, he tells me exactly what he feels. He's great at listening and very straight: if he doesn't like something, he tells me it's rubbish, and if he's not sure he says so, and if he changes his mind he's equally clear about that. He's a wonderful collaborator."

She cites a moment during the making of *Gosford Park*,

for which she also designed the costumes, as an example of his artistic intelligence. "On the first day of shooting he came over to where the costume department was having lunch, and said: 'I've just seen the dailies. They're terrific. I didn't notice the clothes.' That was the biggest compliment he could have made. Clothes are important, but he knows they are just supporting the actors."

As in his film work, Altman invited the actors at the start of rehearsals to improvise a little in the ensemble scenes, suggesting they treat Miller's text as a loose guideline while they became familiar with the story. He's also encouraged them to come up with ideas of their own. "It's the only way I know to work," he says. "I don't have any preconceived notions." Like most directors though, he likes to have some familiar faces in the cast: three of the present company – Jane Adams (*Kansas City*), Matthew Modine (*Short Cuts*) and Neve Campbell (*The Company*) – have appeared in his films, while others such as Maximilian Schell and James Fox have massive screen experience. "Looking around, it's not a typical theatre cast," he admits.

While respecting Miller's text and intentions, he's not averse to making small cuts where necessary, and has even considered changing the scene order. Would he have done this if Miller were alive? "If he were alive I don't think I'd be here," he replies. "I don't think it would have occurred to anyone to ask me to direct the play."

Purpose and Pleasure

After writing about community plays by Ann Jellicoe and Charles Wood, I travelled to Bradford-on-Avon to find out what impact Peter Terson's contribution to the movement,

Under the Fish and Over the Water, *was having on different generations in the Wiltshire town.*

"MY FIRST THOUGHT WAS: it's a hell of a responsibility to write a play for a town. If they weren't proud of it, you'd really be in trouble."

Sixteen months on, playwright Peter Terson is definitely not in trouble. Quite the opposite: his community play for Bradford-on-Avon has brought purpose and pleasure to literally thousands of people in and around this small Wiltshire town. *Under the Fish and Over the Water* has also had a significant effect on the curriculum and on the lives of pupils at St Laurence comprehensive school, the venue for the play's production.

As we sit in the school office before one of the play's twelve performances, Peter Terson talks spiritedly about its effect on the local community. "It's brought together so many people whose lives wouldn't touch otherwise," he says. "People who've been involved have got a terrific lot out of it – and it's been like a Christmas party for the children."

Community plays are based on a simple but powerful formula, whereby a small group of professionals help local people to create an original large-scale play, which celebrates a moment in the community's history. The aim is not just to enable people to develop skills and get to know other people – though both these elements are important – but also to produce, with an essentially amateur cast, a piece of high-quality theatre.

The first community play was put on by playwright Ann Jellicoe in Lyme Regis in 1978. "The idea has become a movement in a way I never imagined," she says. Since the early productions in the West Country, she and others have mounted plays in new towns, parts of London, towns and cities in the Midlands and North, and in Denmark, Canada and the USA. Writers such as Howard Barker, Nick Darke, David Edgar, John Godber, Charles Wood, Adrian Henri, Fay Weldon and Arnold Wesker are among those who have contributed work.

Like most of its predecessors, the Bradford play involves huge numbers of people. Apart from a cast of 160, aged 4-70, many of whom have never acted before, some four hundred people have helped – either backstage, front of house, or in one of the myriad committees set up to fund-raise, seek sponsorship, handle publicity and public relations, or do research. In addition, some 3,500 people saw the play during its two-week run.

The research committee, comprising twenty volunteers, played a crucial part during the writing of the play. They provided the playwright with possible ideas and, once he had chosen his story, travelled far afield, following up leads, researching and checking to ensure the detail was authentic. They also acted as readers for and critics of the various drafts.

The final version skilfully blends fact and fiction, showing the effect of the coming of the machines some two hundred years ago on the lives of individual workers in the local mills, cloth works and quarries. Insurrection is in the air, and a famous riot that took place outside a Bradford clothier's house in 1791 provides a powerful and moving climax to the play.

As with Terson's earlier successes *Zigger Zagger* and *The Apprentices*, which also involved large casts, changes were made to the text right up until the last minute. "Peter sat in on every rehearsal, his dedication was amazing," recalls director Mark Dornford-May. "People would turn up, he'd watch them for a couple of evenings, and then he'd write them into the play."

Pupils at St Laurence say they enjoyed the challenge of working with professionals. "It's been hard work: the director expects a lot more of you than usual," says 14-year-old Stephanie Fisher. A sixth-former, Sophie Blacksell, agrees: "He's quite tough with us, he doesn't allow much for our being amateurs."

Dornford-May, a former assistant director at the Royal Shakespeare Company, believes there is no need to do this: "I've tried to give them the satisfaction of making a good artistic product, and not just having a good time," he says. "With amateurs the skills are the same; you accept that the experience is different. But the enthusiasm, the loyalty and the sense of commitment are greater than in a professional production."

Staff at St Laurence are clear about the beneficial effects of the play for the school, which plans officially to become a community school in April. Headteacher James Wetz says: "Unless your school is involved with the community you might as well shut up shop. The play has brought people together more than any other initiative has. It's also changed relationships and attitudes between staff and children."

There have also been consequences for the curriculum of the school's massive involvement in the play. Adult members of the research committee have shared their findings on the woollen trade with first-year geography pupils. During the run of the play both writer and director worked with A-level theatre studies students, looking at dramatic techniques and text interpretation. And the text itself will be a handy resource in next year's history classes on the industrial revolution.

Reviews of the play are also likely to form part of the coursework for A-level English. Mark James, an English teacher who also chaired the play's steering committee, says: "It's been a real eye-opener: the children have really learnt how a play comes into being, that it's not just a question of somebody sitting down and doing it. We've been able to use that in our work on *A Midsummer Night's Dream.*"

Moira Arthurs, development director of the Colway Trust, which has co-ordinated the professional side of the play, is in no doubt about its success. "With some community plays you wonder what people have gained. With the Bradford one, people's lives have been changed, they've said 'yes' to everything."

Few Bradford people have been untouched by the project. Local businessman Roger Llewellyn says: "It's the first event to bring together the newcomers and those who have lived in the town all their lives. The impact has been fantastic." Darren Woodcock, who works for a local bed manufacturer, and took part in the play, is equally enthusiastic: "Nobody thought it would be this big. I'm so proud it's got to where it has."

In the past community plays have been criticised for raising people's expectations, but leaving nothing for them to build on afterwards. In Bradford there are already plans to film the play, which has been published locally. A public meeting is to be held to discuss future possibilities. As Mark James puts it: "A tremendous amount of energy and expertise has been built up, and we don't want to see that just disappear."

More than a Rehearsal

In the winter of 2009 I spent an absorbing day watching David Suchet, Elizabeth McGovern and Richard Dreyfuss work with director Kevin Spacey on Joe Sutton's play Complicit.

"THAT'S WHAT I LOVE ABOUT this play," says Kevin Spacey. "We have these intense debates, and then I get these guys on their feet, and the drama takes care of itself."

It's an aside made during a lengthy discussion between the director and his actors. Sitting on the floor of the Old Vic's large rehearsal room, they have been hammering out a variety of ideas about American politics of the last forty years. Some directors might call a halt after a few minutes to such an apparent diversion, but Kevin obviously relishes the debate, the chance to hear the actors' ideas, explore his own, and feed them back into the action.

Up to this moment in mid-afternoon, the focus of the day's work has been on sorting out the basic moves for Act 2. It's the start of the second week of rehearsals, and the company of three are at that awkward stage where they half know their lines, but still need their scripts to hand. But they are coping well.

They work initially on the central scene of the act between Ben the journalist (Richard Dreyfuss) and his lawyer Roger (David Suchet), which takes place on the morning of the Grand Jury hearing. It's clear after just a few minutes that both actors are already tapping into the strong emotions that Joe Sutton's text demands. Richard catches convincingly both Ben's arrogance and his angst, while David exudes the strength and authority inherent in Roger's character.

As a director Kevin knows where he wants his actors to

be at given moments, but he allows them flexibility within that framework: "If your instinct is to move earlier, that's fine," he tells Richard at one point. He brings in ideas outside the text, as when he introduces a series of knocks at the door. "I want to up the stakes by making it clear the Grand Jury is assembling next door," he explains. "I want to keep the sense of impending doom, and this will help to drive it."

Likewise, in a scene where Roger and his wife Judy (Elizabeth McGovern) are talking to each other on their mobile phones, he suggests they drop their phones at a certain point, and make direct contact across the stage. It's an imaginative suggestion, and it seems to work. There are lighter moments, and even the odd Hollywood reference; discussing one move Kevin observes: "I want to call it a Robert Redford look-back, but let's call it a Richard Dreyfuss change."

Since the play is being staged in the round, he frequently walks round the edge of the circle marked out as the acting area, to see how the action looks from different viewpoints, to make sure no section of the audience is short-changed. During a break he explains: "You want the play not to be static, to remain moving and fluid, but you don't want it to look staged. It only really works if the audience doesn't notice. You want it to feel that when people move there's a reason for moving. And I think after *The Norman Conquests* the audience will be a little bit used to the idea that you can watch a scene and for a time have someone's back to you, and actually not lose anything. It can be a very strong thing: it's what happens all the time in real life."

Sometimes as they work he whispers an idea to one actor, to see how the others react without knowing what he has said. He spends a lot of time inside the circle, guiding the actors to their next positions, suggesting what might be an appropriate distance between them. Often he watches them intently from just three or four feet away, seeming at times almost to be part of the action, to share their fluctuating emotions.

They move on next to the emotional scene between Ben and Judy. Elizabeth conveys well Judy's distress at the dilemma Ben is facing. Although it's tough for both actors to play this climactic moment, lying on the floor while having occasionally to check the text, the scene is already gaining considerable shape and conviction. There's a pause while Kevin explains why he's decided to make a couple of significant cuts near its climax. "These lines feel like a distraction from the drama," he says. "They're informational stuff that I don't care about at this stage. The audience already knows what the context is: what matters here is the personal drama."

Further questions arise and provoke discussion. Will Ben survive as a result of his choice of action? Should the audience be given an indication of why he did it, or be left to decide for themselves? And will his and Judy's fractured relationship endure?

At this point Elizabeth raises a specific question about Judy's relationship with Ben. This leads gradually to a sustained and wide-ranging debate between the three of them about political issues in the 1960s and 1970s, covering topics such as student protest, the Vietnam war, political idealism and cynicism, flower power, and many other aspects of recent American history. For a while it feels more like a university seminar than a play rehearsal.

At one stage Kevin throws in the parallel case of Elia Kazan, the film director who betrayed his communist colleagues and named names to the House Un-American

Activities Committee. "Why did he do it?" he asks. "Did he think he wouldn't work again if he didn't? Or did he never ask the kind of moral questions that Ben does?" Richard suggests: "He was anti-communist, and a serial betrayer."

The debate eventually segues into a further analysis of Judy's role in her marriage, and how far she is given the chance to articulate the crucial arguments with Ben. David then rejoins them as they return to the text for a final session. By the end of the day a good deal of ground has been covered. Kevin is pleased with progress. "I can see the ideas and arcs are getting into your brains," he tells the actors. "'There's a strong sense of where you're going, and that's very encouraging."

Tangled Relationships

Kevin Spacey began his inaugural season as artistic director of the Old Vic by directing Cloaca, *a dark comedy about male friendships by the Dutch writer Maria Goos. During a break in rehearsals he and his actors – Hugh Bonneville, Neil Pearson, Stephen Tomkinson, Adrian Lukis and Ingeborga Dapkunaite – talked to me about their characters and the motivation for their behaviour.*

"SHE HAS OBSERVED THE MALE psyche at close quarters, and encapsulated it brilliantly in dramatic form. I don't think a man could have written it so perceptively."

Hugh Bonneville is not the only member of the *Cloaca* company to feel that Maria Goos has skewered the male sex in her bleakly comic play. As they explore their individual characters during rehearsals, he and his fellow-actors talk of the playwright's ability to pin down the ambitions, delusions, betrayals and disappointments of her middle-aged male characters, all of whom experience emotional crises during the action. Yet they are also quick to point out the objectivity, compassion and generosity with which she has drawn her characters.

Stephen Tompkinson plays Pieter, a neat, fastidious and gay civil servant, in whose flat the action takes place. "He can provide something in his space that the others can't get from their own lives," he says. "He's the referee between everyone else's squabbles, the comfort buffer-zone. He provides a sounding-board for them, a kind of agony aunt, someone to confess to and chill out with before they get on with their own lives. He's very good at observing, but he likes to do it from a distance. He's worked out a way of living that he's happy with. He's a loner, but a very disciplined one. I think he's a sympathetic and very sensitive character."

Neil Pearson has the role of Marten, an avant-garde theatre director. "If you take him at his own estimation, he's at the cutting edge of theatre," he explains. "So it comes as a shock to him to hear what his friends now think of his work. What old friends can do is take the gloves off, tell it like it is, and make you confront aspects of yourself that you may be reluctant to admit to yourself. In the past he has been the fun liaison officer, but now he's running out of ideas, both professionally and privately. He hates his failure with women, and this shows itself in his very unpleasant misogyny."

Adrian Lukis plays Tom, a coke-snorting, manic-depressive lawyer. "It's a very interesting part," he observes. "Although he is vulnerable, he's not passive or meek, he's quite prepared to tell the others that they are all losers. He's survived his earlier crisis, but he's on lithium, he's obviously unstable, and I think he's quite fragile; he doesn't know what's real any more. He used to be fun, the kind of guy who would suggest flying to Paris on an impulse, but the cocaine tipped him over the edge, and now he's lost it all."

Hugh Bonneville is cast as Jan the politician, possibly the most unpleasant character in the play. "He's ruthlessly ambitious," he suggests, "and his eye for the main chance has badly affected his marriage. He's a career politician rather than an ideological one, and convinced of his own worth – it's his friends who suggest he's not as great as he thinks he is. I see shades of Mandelson and Blair and New Labour: with him it's all about presentation and personality, not policy. Yet like all the characters, he's complicated: the most wonderful moment of his life is the birth of his daughter."

Ingeborga Dapkunaite plays the mysterious woman who dramatically enters the lives of the reunited friends. "The play has so many themes: even in my character's story there is attachment, betrayal, love and survival," she explains. "Maria's view of men is very humorous, and you certainly recognise the types and their behaviour, which makes it very enjoyable. It's based on her own experience, a compilation of people she knows, so perhaps that's why they seem so real."

As director, Kevin Spacey relishes the nuances and the variety to be found in the behaviour of the four friends. "It's interesting the way in which we learn how each feels about the other, sometimes in the form of an attack, sometimes in the form of humour, sometimes from something that's just thrown away. But we do get a sense that they've all known each other for a long time; there's this fantastic undercurrent of knowledge. I'm very moved by the entanglements of the relationships: it's a web, but it's an accessible one, it doesn't feel murky."

In working on the text the actors have been pondering what has kept the friends together for more than twenty years. "For each of them, the other three represent the best chance they have of being understood, or being accepted, and of their responsibilities to other people outside their circle," Neil Pearson suggests. "It's also their shared history, which is one of fun and optimism about the future, and supporting each other in the bad times and enjoying the good ones." Stephen Tompkinson feels that Pieter has remained at the heart of the group "because he reminds the others of what they were when they were students. He's the only one who has remained on his own – though his digs have got better."

The actors have also been enjoying the flexibility of their characters. Adrian Lukis observes: "If you write psychologically true dialogue, the parts can be played in many different ways. Hamlet can be played by a million different actors, and in a similar way Maria has created recognisable types. But she's not nailed them down so much that only a certain kind of actor can play each role."

Hugh Bonneville is in no doubt that many in the audience will find themselves looking in a mirror reflecting their own lives. "It's a very funny play, but it will be the laughter of painful recognition. I think there will be a few blokes in the audience squirming, with their wives or girlfriends prodding them and saying, 'That's you!' "

4

Adaptations

All About My Mother – The New Statesman

All About Rehearsals

In the autumn of 2007 Samuel Adamson wrote All About My Mother, *a play based on Pedro Almodóvar's celebrated film. When I visited rehearsals at the Old Vic, a company that included Lesley Manville, Mark Gatiss, Eleanor Bron and Diana Rigg were starting to shift into a higher gear.*

THREE WEEKS AGO, AT THE read-through, the actors played it cool, restrained, tentative, wary of showing too much too soon. Today, more than half way through their rehearsal period, they are at another level, and starting to give the powerful emotions of Samuel Adamson's characters something like their full expression.

The room at the top of the Old Vic is now cluttered with furniture, clothes and props, with temporary blocks of chipwood standing in for scenery. The floor is marked with a confusing series of coloured lines and marks, identifying the many sets that the fast-flowing action of *All About My Mother* will require.

"We've got to the stage of linking the scenes together for the first time, and that's a complex business," director Tom Cairns explains. And so it proves: a lot of time is spent during the day working on the vital mechanics of scene changes, on deciding who shifts props and scenery, and how. But in between there is still time to focus on the text itself, and work through several scenes from the top.

In the opening one, where a simulation is taking place in a hospital, Lesley Manville as Manuela goes into top emotional gear with impressive immediacy. Tom voices concern about the scene's visual look. "It's going to hit the audience left-field, so we have to make absolutely clear the distinction between the exercise and real life." Some significant move changes help to achieve this when they repeat the scene.

The warm but complex relationship between Manuela and her son Esteban (Colin Morgan) is nicely established in the following scene, although Tom suggests that the actors "could ping it out to us a bit more". He's an intense, instinctive and witty man, who creates a merry, relaxed atmosphere in the rehearsal room. His directing style is gently persuasive, his suggestions to the actors often accompanied by remarks such as "If you feel you can", or "Would you mind trying that?"

For the first of the brief scenes from *A Streetcar Named Desire* which are inserted into the story, there is a need to establish the exact boundaries of the set for the play within a play. The actors had the benefit a few days ago of doing a read-through of Tennessee Williams' classic work, so they could see their fragmented scenes in their proper context. Today Diana Rigg (Huma Rojo) makes a touchingly vulnerable Blanche DuBois, while Charlotte Randle (Nina Cruz) and Bradley Freegard (Mario Del Toro) already seem at ease playing Stella and Stanley Kowalski.

One of the more difficult scenes to crack is set outside the theatre where *Streetcar* is playing, with Esteban waiting in the hope of getting Huma Rojo's autograph, and simultaneously interrogating Manuela to try and discover the truth about his father. Tom and Colin work on getting right the balance between these two pulls on Esteban's attention, while also ensuring that the actors emerging from the theatre do so spot on cue. "Don't forget that there will be a lot of atmosphere at this moment, with rain falling, and car headlights beaming across the set," Tom reminds them.

Here and at other moments of the day he looks for a second opinion about a scene from Samuel Adamson, who sits unobtrusively behind him at the back of the room. "I enjoy coming to rehearsals, but I choose my moments," the playwright says. "Sometimes you just need to stay away so the actors can get on with it, without the feeling that they're being judged." He and Tom spent a lot of time discussing the script before rehearsals began, and have clearly built up a good working relationship. "We trust each other, so we can both give our thoughts an airing. We can talk honestly about the script or the rehearsal, and not give offence."

After lunch it's the turn of Mark Gatiss as Agrado, a transvestite, already resplendent in his/her costume of silver shoes, thick brown tights, light blue shorts and a T-shirt. He delivers his speech at the theatre, entertaining the audience with the story of his life in Barcelona's red-light district. It's very high camp but subtly done, in a lilting Welsh accent that seems to fit the part well.

Then we're into his apartment and his surprise meeting with Manuela. This and other settings have been inspired in part by the arresting photographs of Nan Goldin featured in her book *The Devil's Playground*, notably shots of women, hospitals and cityscapes. Copies of several images have been stuck on the back wall by set designer Hildegard Bechtler, next to a good-luck message from Almodóvar ("See you in a month – until then hugs and kisses to all").

Next comes the Agrado-Manuela scene, the longest yet, giving the two actors the chance to unfold their characters' love for each other. At this stage Tom is picking them up on small technical details rather than psychological points. At one moment the two actors play what is clearly a game from the past, in which they pretend to be dogs barking. "It's not clear at first what sound you're making," Tom says. "We need a barking workshop." They try it again, and are convincingly canine.

The last scene of the day involves Manuela and Agrado's visit to the nunnery, and their meeting with Sister Rosa (Joanne Froggatt), the nun who works with transvestites. This runs smoothly enough after being played twice, prompting Tom to announce: "Let's do something shocking and run those last three scenes together." The result, while throwing up a few obvious technical problems, is satisfyingly up to speed. "It's coming on nicely," Tom observes, and calls it a day for the actors.

Afterwards director and writer have a brief post-mortem on the day's work. For Samuel Adamson these are useful occasions, a chance to focus on the positive. "I wanted Tom to know that I was pleased with the way certain scenes were going, the way the actors were finding new things in my text. I think it's important to do this, to focus on the positive things as well as on the problems still to be solved."

A Right B'Stard

Following his success as the evil unscrupulous politician in the television series The New Statesman, *Rik Mayall brought Alan B'Stard on to the stage in 2007. I met him in a West End theatre while he was rehearsing for a nationwide tour.*

RIK MAYALL BANGS THE TABLE with his fist. "This is not a stage version of a very old telly show. This is a play about *now*." Then Alan B'Stard fixes me with a manic gaze. "It came about because I'm a patriot: whenever the nation is in crisis, that's when I come to the help of my country. It's why I'm on the planet. People were suffering under Thatcher, so I removed her. Now it's Blair's turn, so I'm back."

There are apparently three people in this interview. But Rik Mayall happily admits, as we talk before rehearsals for his new show, that he shares many characteristics with Alan B'Stard, the unscrupulous Tory politician from the television series *The New Statesman*, who is about to make his stage debut. "Alan is that aspect of myself that is posh, selfish, evil, manipulative, nasty, and very funny," he says proudly. "He's a fantastic character, and a joy to play."

It was Maurice Gran and Laurence Marks, the creators of *The New Statesman*, who suggested putting the deliciously offensive politician on the stage. "Their script came out of the blue," Mayall says. "I was thrilled, because I see the theatre as the last bastion of free speech. Nowadays the BBC is just a mouthpiece for the government; it wouldn't allow three-quarters of the jokes in the play to be made on television."

It was of course television where the comic actor first made his mark in the early 1980s, initially with *The Comic Strip* and *A Kick up the Eighties*, then as Rik in *The Young Ones*, which made him a household name. In 1987 came *The New Statesman*, and the chance to bring his wild and anarchic and occasionally violent talents to the amoral character that is B'Stard who, despite heavy competition in the real world, must be one of the nastiest British politicians to disgrace the Westminster stage.

B'Stard, whom Mayall modestly describes as "a national treasure", has apparently been very busy in recent years. "Once he had bankrupted everyone in the Conservative Party, he crossed the floor of the House. He then destroyed Old Labour, and recreated the party in the true Conservative image. He found an ignorant eunuch from a public school called Tony Blair, and moulded him into a prime minister, and then filled the party with the young, posh yuppies and blonde women. So now we have two Conservative parties, with Alan installed at number nine Downing Street, giving Tony orders."

While he is reluctant to give away the plot of the new show, let alone the jokes, Mayall is willing to lift the curtain a little. Although much of the comic focus will again be on the sleaze and machinations at Westminster, B'Stard is now evidently a figure on the world stage, and heavily into global politics. "So there's a lot of oil, a lot of war, a lot of assassination and kidnapping, and a lot of dealings with Bush, Condoleeza Rice, Gaddafi and other Middle East people. We also wanted Osama bin Laden to be in it, but his agent couldn't find him."

Because of the play's topical element, parts of the script

are frequently having to be changed. Already several Lib Dem gags have gone, as Charles Kennedy's drink problem and his potential successors' sexual preferences have become last week's news. But the rewrites won't stop once the show opens. "It's a rolling, organic play," Mayall stresses. "The boys are coming on the road, so when something happens they'll hand me a new gag or line. It's all very exciting. It's also the public's last chance to see something really good: because of global warming, three-quarters of British theatres are soon going to be under water."

Although describing himself as "not a proper actor", because he wasn't formally trained, he has nevertheless appeared in Brecht, Beckett and Shakespeare, and played the title-role in Gogol's *The Government Inspector* at the National. More recently he was in Simon Gray's *Cell Mates* and Noël Coward's *Present Laughter*. "But I'm a little intimidated by the classics, because of all the people who've done them so well. New plays are another matter."

Playing Alan B'Stard is, he confesses, therapeutic. "Fundamentally it's a kind of exorcism of the things I disapprove of about myself. Acting is like drinking, it's being out of your head. It's a rest from being yourself."

He's not been on the road for three years, since touring *Bottom* with Adrian Edmondson. "I love working in the theatre, because the audience is your best director. They tell you what they like and what they don't like. You don't have to bother about someone else stopping you and telling you what you should be doing differently."

5

Musicals and Pantomimes

My Fair Lady – A Little Night Music –
Aladdin – Cinderella

Will It Be Loverly?

With Jonathan Pryce cast as Professor Higgins and Martine McCutcheon a surprise choice for Eliza Doolittle, choreographer Matthew Bourne outlined to me his plans for Trevor Nunn's 2001 National production of My Fair Lady.

MIX THE FOUNDER OF THE ground-breaking dance company Adventures in Motion Pictures with the great *Pygmalion*-inspired Lerner and Loewe musical, and you'd think you'd get a gender-bending, subversive makeover. But if that's your expectation, you could be in for a surprise.

"I've never really felt like a radical choreographer,"

Matthew Bourne explains, as we talk just before rehearsals begin. "It's just that the form I've been working in with Adventures in Motion Pictures is quite unusual. My real interest is in storytelling, and being very clear and entertaining. My viewpoint on things is actually quite old-fashioned."

He sees *My Fair Lady* as very much a period piece, set in a particular world. "It's certainly not going to be a radical take on it. I don't think you can do a modern version, because it just wouldn't work. So we're doing it absolutely in period. But it's also a very fifties musical, with songs such as 'On the Street Where You Live' being sung before a front cloth while the set is being changed. The challenge is to make it more like a modern musical, so you travel between sets in a more organic way."

Musicals are in Matthew Bourne's bloodstream. Brought up in Walthamstow, where he went to the local comprehensive, he can't remember a time when he wasn't aware of them. The first film he saw was *The Sound of Music*, at the age of five. "My parents loved musicals, so they just sat me in front of the television whenever one was on." According to his mother, he could pick up songs before he could put sentences together. Later he graduated to musicals in the West End. "I was a regular man-about-town by about 14," he remembers.

Now 40, in addition to his celebrated reworking of classics such as *Nutcracker*, *Swan Lake* and *Cinderella*, he's choreographed other musicals – *Oliver!*, directed by Sam Mendes, *Children of Eden* with John Caird, and *Showboat*. But *My Fair Lady* may be his last production solely as choreographer.

"I'm much more interested in combining directing and choreographing, in having the whole vision. But I didn't want to turn down the chance of working with Trevor. I've always learnt a lot from the directors I've worked with, ideas that I've brought back to my dancing, such as the need for everyone on stage to have a life-story. Too often in dance or musicals the chorus just comes on and stands around, not knowing who they are and why they are there."

He's pleased that, while the Olivier might have been the more obvious theatre in which to stage *My Fair Lady*, it's actually to be played in the Lyttelton. "Everyone thinks a choreographer wants wide open spaces, but I don't like them. I like to pack a set, so dancers have objects to use in an interesting environment."

Shaw's famous story of the flower girl being passed off as a princess also appeals to him because it's set in the city he knows and loves. "I'm a very English choreographer, with very English loves and influences. I often play with social class and observation in my own work, and of course that's at the heart of *My Fair Lady*."

In that respect he's looking forward to seeing how Martine McCutcheon fares as Eliza. "The part has usually been played by well-spoken actresses such as Julie Andrews or, in the film, Audrey Hepburn. Because they've been rather a prettified flower girl, they've always had trouble with the first half. Martine will have no trouble whatsoever on that score. With her it's the right way round, so the transformation will be all the greater."

Where the production *will* be radical, he believes, is in its interpretation of the story. "What Trevor has done so fantastically, with *Oklahoma!* and other musicals that he's reinvented, is to get to the real essence of it, and not just accept what has gone before. That's what's going to make it a really interesting experience for me."

The Making of a Show

Sean Mathias' production of Stephen Sondheim's A Little Night Music *became one of the most successful shows in the National's history. During its long run in 1995-96, I looked at how the many people involved combined to bring the famous musical to life.*

PLAYS AT THE NATIONAL COME in all shapes and sizes. Even the sparest production in the small Cottesloe auditorium needs extensive planning and sustained cooperation between individuals and departments. When it comes to a big musical in the Olivier, the demands are greater and the stakes higher. How then did the many departments of the National, a large and complex institution, come together to create the hugely successful production of Sondheim's *A Little Night Music*?

The show came about because Sean Mathias had recently had a success at the National directing Jean Cocteau's *Les Parents Terribles*, and the theatre's director Richard Eyre asked him what he might like to do next. His first thought was something staged in cabaret style, but further discussions led to the idea of reviving Sondheim's classic musical, based on Ingmar Bergman's dark romantic comedy film *Smiles of a Summer Night*. The National had already staged Sondheim's *Sunday in the Park with George* (1990) and *Sweeney Todd* (1993), and the time seemed ripe for a revival of *A Little Night Music*.

Before making the decision, the National's management had to take into account plans for two other Sondheim musicals, *Passion* and *Company*, which they knew might be staged in the West End at about the same time. In the end it was felt that their presence would be more beneficial than harmful, in part because *A Little Night Music* was reckoned to be the most accessible of the three works. Besides, it would fit in well with other productions in the repertoire: Jonson's *Volpone*, Brecht's *Mother Courage and Her Children* and Tony Harrison's *The Prince's Play* (based on Victor Hugo's *Le Roi s'amuse*) would provide the right weighty balance and contrast to the astringent romanticism of the Sondheim piece.

Balancing the Budget

Once the artistic decision had been made, financial matters had to be tackled – so the head of planning and the finance department looked at such crucial questions as the length and timing of the run, the possibility of a tour, the availability of the preferred artists, ticket pricing, the likely cost and the likely income. After discussions with the casting and music departments, and an assessment of the fees for the director, designer, actors and musicians, a production budget for the show was built up, and fitted into the theatre's overall budget for 1995-96. Final approval was given by the National's board, with executive director Genista McIntosh having the responsibility for any overspending. In the case of *A Little Night Music*, a generous donation from the Mackintosh Foundation made the production possible.

Creating the Team

Decisions about the creative team are usually made jointly by the show's director and Richard Eyre. For Sean Mathias some choices were straightforward. He had already collaborated with the designer Stephen Brimson Lewis on four plays, including *Les Parents Terribles*, while Paddy Cunneen had been the music director on *Sweeney Todd*. In casting musicals you have to look for people who can sing, dance and act. At least ten people were auditioned for each of the subsidiary parts.

The decision to use Laurence Guittard in the leading part of Fredrik posed a problem. All members of non-EU countries need a work permit, and the actors' union Equity was reluctant to allow a foreign actor to take a role that could be filled by a British actor. But an exchange scheme was agreed between British and American Equity: Jude Law had recently appeared in the National's production of *Les Parents Terribles* on Broadway, so in return Guittard could appear in London.

In the Olivier you have to ensure that 1,200 people can hear every word and instrument. The art lies in perfecting the sound system so that the audience are unaware of any amplification. Achieving this was not easy, even on the show's sound budget of £40,000. Specialist speakers and other equipment had to be bought to reinforce the system and achieve the correct balance.

The music department already had contact with a pool of musicians, but with *A Little Night Music* care had to be taken to select performers who would not mind being on stage throughout the performance. An early question to be settled between the creative team and the sound, lighting and music managers was where to put the eighteen musicians. The initial idea to create an orchestra pit was rejected on both cost and visual grounds, and because it would mean losing seats at the front of the auditorium. In the end the band occupied a curved, five-tier tower at one side of the stage, which became effectively part of the set.

As for lighting, various ways were explored of creating

special effects such as a moon, clouds, and the midnight sun. Many technical problems had to be overcome: sometimes ten ideas were tested before the right solution was found. Because extra was being spent on sound, it was even more important for the set to be kept within budget. Initially the designer wanted an enormous tree centre stage, but this was clearly impossible to move during the twenty-minute interval. The two vintage cars bringing the guests to their weekend in the country were at first going to be fully motorised, but in the end only pedals could be afforded. And the magnificent, apparently authentic period chandelier was in fact created out of aluminium, cardboard, plastic, and jam jars and glasses found in a charity shop.

Into Rehearsal

Musicals always take longer to rehearse than straight plays. *A Little Night Music* took seven weeks. During the technical rehearsal, when the production moved out of the rehearsal rooms and on to the stage, the needs of the actors had to be subordinated for a while to ensure the technical side was working smoothly. Four days were needed for the "tech", and many late changes were made.

The big problem was taming the machinery. The set worked very well, but getting the foundations in order was difficult. The Olivier's drum revolve, for instance – on which whole sets can be swirled down to forty feet below the stage, be replaced, and the next set swirled up – can be hard to manage. Eventually it worked perfectly, but the tech was so complex that no time was left for a full dress rehearsal. During the week of previews the technicians and creative team were still refining the show. Finally all was set for the first night.

During rehearsals, and in some cases well before, many other members of the National had been busy. Because so many tickets had to be sold, the marketing campaign had begun earlier than usual. A promotional leaflet was sent to the 40,000 people on the National's mailing list. Advertisements were taken in the national daily and Sunday papers and – on the basis that most spending decisions are made by women – in several glossy women's magazines. Space was also taken in publications not normally used by the National, such as the *Mail on Sunday*, to attract first-time visitors. And a full-colour programme was compiled and designed.

A Gala Evening

Just before the opening night a Royal Gala performance was held, attended by Princess Alexandra. The aim was to raise money for the National Theatre Foundation, and attract new donors. The gala itself was sponsored by £50,000 from SRGent, the clothing company, as part of its fiftieth-anniversary celebrations. Nearly 900 tickets were sold at between £25 and £250. Key figures from the National's Development Council, such as Lady Greenbury and James Benfield, persuaded commercial and business leaders to pay for sixteen corporate tables, each costing £15,000.

The National's catering department pursued the idea of a "themed" evening. Research was undertaken into Swedish food and drink such as schnapps and smorgasbord, and £10,000 worth of decorative flowers were chosen to mirror the reds and lilacs on the set of the show. Some guests dined in the Lyttelton exhibition area; others in the Mezzanine restaurant; others still in a marquee erected on the terrace; and the rest of the night's audience were given champagne and canapés.

Earlier the same evening Stephen Sondheim himself was interviewed on the Lyttelton stage in front of a sell-out audience. This was one of several Platforms – the National's early evening programme of literary, cultural and publishing events – that were linked to the production or cast of *A Little Night Music*.

A Hit on their Hands

By the opening night it was clear that the National had a commercial hit on their hands, since the show's first two-month booking period was already sold out. In the following weeks the theatre's thirty box-office staff often received as many as two thousand calls a day – twice the normal number. It was evident from the questions people were asking – Where is the National? Can I have a box? What should I wear? – that many more of the audience than usual were coming to the National for the first time.

A few weeks into the run, well before Christmas 1995, a crucial decision was taken. Because of the show's success, it was decided not only to extend its run, but to end it the following summer with a straight run of eight performances a week for six weeks. This broke the normal pattern of the National's repertory system, but for a good reason. The demand for seats was overwhelming, but with the repertory system you can't book beyond a certain date. The public was finding that difficult to understand, since it was obvious the show would be running on for quite a while. The booking period was therefore extended, so that from February the public was able to book seats from the beginning of April through to the end of the run.

There were other implications. How many of the cast

would be prepared to stay? The vast majority agreed, helped by the offer of a ten-day summer break before the straight run. In the marketing department, a relaunch budget of £45,000 was earmarked well in advance, allowing a poster campaign to be mounted in the London Underground to catch the summer tourists.

The National is unlike the West End, in that even an exceptionally successful show can't run for ever, and certainly for no more than a year. By the end of its run *A Little Night Music* will have had 212 performances. But it will not completely disappear once it leaves the repertoire; the show will live on in another medium.

Although three recordings of the musical are already available, the National has negotiated a deal to produce yet another version, this time with the Olivier cast. The company spent three days recording the show in a London studio. So Sondheim *aficionados* and thousands of others who came to the South Bank now have the chance to own a permanent record of one of the most successful shows in the National's history.

Two Times Aladdin

For the Old Vic's Christmas pantomime in 2004, Sean Mathias directed Ian McKellen, Roger Allam and Maureen Lipman in a new version of the famous story. I talked to the company and creative team about the original production, then returned the following year to watch them rehearse the revival.

New Gags for Old

STANDING IN THE WINGS OF the Grand Theatre, Bolton, a stage-struck lad marvels at the comics and magicians, the chorus girls and acrobats performing on the music-hall stage. Some fifty years later, having reached the theatrical heights and attained international screen stardom, Ian McKellen is fulfilling a long-held dream.

"I think everybody has some ideal about what a pantomime should be, and it's probably the first one they saw. I went to many of them in my childhood, first with my parents, who had to hold me back when children were invited up on the stage, and then by myself. I've always thought it a wonderful form, because it can include anything the theatre is able to give a welcome to. For years I kept asking myself why I wasn't playing in one. The answer was there was no opportunity. Eventually I realised I'd have to create my own."

How did the McKellen dream become a reality? How did this renowned Shakespearean actor come to be fooling around in frocks in a theatre best known for staging the classics? Shortly before rehearsals of *Aladdin* began I talked to the show's creative team and principal actors, to find out how this talented group of artists was putting together a spanking new version of this ancient fable.

The story begins with McKellen himself. In his early days in rep at Ipswich he had played a Chinese policeman in *Aladdin*. Now, having also considered *Cinderella* and *Mother Goose*, he decided to stage the same show, with himself as the Dame, Widow Twankey. As a first step he read and digested several versions of the story. Then, at the 2004 Sydney Theatre Festival, he met the writer and actor Bille Brown, an old friend whose work included the RSC's panto *The Swan Down Gloves*. A true pantomime buff, Brown asked to be adviser on the project, but McKellen suggested he should write it, and commissioned a treatment.

After studying various versions and adaptations from different periods, Brown produced a rough draft. The Old Vic snapped him up. "It showed great trust on Kevin Spacey's part," McKellen admits. "To an American, pantomime is as mysterious as cricket. When I explained it to him his face misted over. Then he laughed, and said: "I don't know what it's going to be, but you must do it!"

The Old Vic then offered it to director Sean Mathias, who accepted, but without being able to see a proper script. "This was daunting, because normally it's the text that unlocks my creative imagination," he says. "But when it arrived I thought it was great. Because it's inspired by a version of *The Arabian Nights* it has a romantic quality. It also has a very strong story, and because I'm used to narrative that made me feel I could do it."

His chosen set designer was John Napier who, long before working on *Cats*, *Starlight Express*, *Les Misérables* and other glittering West End shows, had designed the celebrated McKellen/Dench *Macbeth* with a budget of just £250. This proved an excellent calling-card for the Old Vic show. "Pantos are often a bit tacky scenically," Napier says. "The challenge with this *Aladdin* was to do something terrific but on a shoestring. You have to use your imagination in a different way."

The first design idea emerged from discussions between designer and director. "Although the story is set in China, it takes us to a number of other places," Mathias points out. "I wondered how we could represent these places without using the traditional pantomime crafts, and also make it

Chinese. I had this notion of a red lacquered box; John liked the idea, and ran with it."

While pondering what style to use for the sets, Napier had a "eureka" moment. "Flo Perry, the daughter of a family who were neighbours of mine, had done a watercolour drawing of my house. I was looking at it one evening, and suddenly realised she might be the key. Her drawings were strange, very childlike, but also clever. I thought they would be a good basis for something fresh."

He commissioned Flo, now twelve, to make some black-and-white drawings, which he then cut up, re-pasted and coloured. Their collaboration grew as the idea proved fruitful: first she drew the front cloth, then Widow Twankey's washing line, next the Emperor's palace, and eventually the finale curtain. "Originally I tried to draw them myself, but my versions were horrible, much too architectural," Napier says. "Flo's were delicate and beautiful. She's been a true inspiration." Flo, who intends to be a fashion designer, adds: "John says my drawings have got a naive sophistication, but I don't really know what that means."

Flo has also done several costume sketches, providing a jumping-off point for the costume designer. "They got me looking for images that relate to her vision as well as to John's sets," costume designer Mark Bouman explains. "I found contemporary photos of Japanese and Chinese kids dressing really creatively for the street, which could be the inspiration for the ensemble." With around a hundred costumes to design, ten of them for Widow Twankey, he's been uncovering many Chinese and Arabian images in books and museums.

For composer Gareth Valentine, Aladdin has proved rich in musical possibilities. "It's a really good story to write a score for," he says. "I wanted the numbers to be as diverse as possible, so I treated it rather like a box of confectionery." The flavours on offer in his witty and brilliantly varied score include 1940s swing music, grand opera, a touch of Gilbert and Sullivan, a Broadway moment, a hint of *Madame Butterfly*, jazz, ballet music, a pastiche of *Sheherazade*, and a piece based on his own Requiem Mass.

A lot of the music is gleaned from the Middle East, and some of it is akin to Jewish music. He has now sent the score to Chris Walker for orchestration. "I have in mind a lot of Chinese sounds, percussive ones like tam tam gongs, finger cymbals and Chinese mouth organs." He's also been working on the lyrics. "Bille Brown's script included some lyrics, but really just as a guide. I've had *carte blanche* to rework them, and with some numbers to invent them from scratch. Ian and Sean have also had a hand in writing them, so we've all thrown our bit in, which has been great fun." But one song will not be theirs: when McKellen and Mathias spoke about the show to Elton John at an Oscars party, he agreed to write a love song for it. "We shook hands on it in the balmy Hollywood air," McKellen recalls.

The choreography for the ten numbers is the responsibility of Wayne McGregor, who runs Random Dance, the resident company at Sadler's Wells. With only three weeks in which to rehearse he is having to map out certain ideas in advance. "Using Gareth's score, I'm discussing them with Sean. But really you need to have the actors there, so things might change radically in rehearsal. After all, the thing about panto is for the actors to get their personalities over, so I want to encourage them to physicalise their characters so they communicate properly."

Casting the ensemble has been one of the toughest tasks, he says. He and Mathias saw more than two hundred people in order to select just eight. "We got there in the end, but it took a long time to find the right balance. Those who are first-class dancers can't necessarily sing very well, while those with good voices aren't always the best movers. And that's without considering their acting ability, for the chosen eight will understudy the principals."

While the creative team was busy the script was being worked on collaboratively by the show's writer, director and star. "It's like a Christmas pudding, we all get a stir," Bille Brown observes. He recalls that the idea of Twankey's show-business ambitions had its origins in McKellen's Lancashire background. "Ian talked about the tradition of amateur dramatics in the north and about his passion for the theatre." But the idea also resonated with Mathias, whose mother, an amateur actress, loved to play the Dame in her village hall.

Casting the other three principal roles proved easier than expected. For Abbanazar, Mathias and McKellen were looking for a classical actor who could sing, catch the pantomime villain's dark and menacing quality, but also play light, have a sense of fun, and handle the camp element. Their first choice, Roger Allam – whose roles have included Javert in *Les Misérables*, Capt Dennis in *Privates on Parade* and Willy Brandt in *Democracy* – fulfilled all these requirements.

Although Sam Kelly, cast as the Emperor of China, has considerable pantomime experience – he's played Wishee Washee twice in *Aladdin*, and been in *Cinderella* and *Robinson Crusoe* – he was essentially chosen on the basis of his delicious performance in *A Funny Thing Happened on the Way to the Forum*. "I always thought he was a bit of a comic genius, a very good actor with great musicality," Mathias says. 'Then Ian and I saw him in *Forum*, laughed a great deal, and that was it."

Finding their Dim Sum – usually known as Wishee Washee – was a little more complicated. The original idea was to have a male actor. "But then I read the script again," Mathias recalls, "and had this instinct that it would be wonderful played by a woman." Since Aladdin was to be a male rather than a female principal boy, McKellen also supported the idea of a bit of extra cross-dressing. "We made up a list, and just then Maureen Lipman rang to ask if there was a part for her. The answer was yes."

Like McKellen, Maureen Lipman has had her *Aladdin* moment, as the Genie of the Ring at the Watford Palace in 1969. "I had a blue frizzy wig, John Lennon glasses, lots of beads and bangles, and I entered on a pogo stick," she remembers. "It was great fun and absolutely exhausting." Roger Allam, a former Sheriff of Nottingham in *Babes in the Wood* at the Glasgow Citizens, found the experience liberating, and is looking forward to playing another pantomime villain. "I hope there will be many chances to overact," he says. "The opportunity to change appearance and disappear through trapdoors is immensely appealing." For Sam Kelly too it's a chance to let his hair down: "You have to treat it seriously at first, but then you can go a little mad."

Amidst all this intense and high-level creativity, it's apparent that everyone is also having enormous fun. As rehearsals loom, the main players are clearly relishing the work. "It's wonderful to be doing something which requires such lightness and wit," Mathias says. "I hope it will really brighten up Christmas in London." McKellen has similar hopes: "It's all a bit of an adventure for me. In a pantomime there's a wider variety of pure theatre than you get even in Shakespeare. And if it works, it's unforgettable."

Hello Boys and Girls

"Can you catch bird flu from Toilet Duck?" asks Dim Sum, aka Frances Barber. It's a typical moment in a gag-filled, high-octane day at the end of the first week of rehearsals. Guided by director Sean Mathias, the *Aladdin* company works with obvious enjoyment and great intensity on three songs, two dance numbers, a chase, and three dialogue scenes.

This is a remodelled version of last year's original production. Apart from the addition of the usual topical jokes, the story has been clarified, there have been music and lyrics changes, certain characters have been strengthened, while cast changes bring in a new Dim Sum, Aladdin and Princess.

In a smallish, low-ceilinged room near the Old Vic, the rehearsal begins with Dim Sum and the Emperor (Paul Grunert) working on the traditional "song sheet" routine. This part of the script, where the actors are talking directly to the audience, is still open to negotiation. A couple of gags are offered by the actors: one is accepted, the other Sean rates "too risqué for the kids". This is a constant dilemma: where to draw the line with the bawdy humour in front of a mixed-age audience.

Next, musical director Kevin Amos takes the ensemble through the beautiful requiem song "Peace and Justice". No gags here, just a meticulous concern with getting all the nuances right. Kevin ensures that every comma is expressed, every consonant properly articulated. The result is impressive, and already very moving.

Aladdin and the Princess then rehearse their first meeting. Even dressed casually in tracksuit and jeans, Neil McDermott and Kate Gillespie manage to put over bags of youthful charm and sincerity, which continue to be in evidence in their romantic duet "I Believe in You", written specially for the show by Elton John.

Next we're into the chase of Aladdin by the two dim-witted policemen, Hanky and Panky. New to their parts, Matthew Wolfenden and Andrew Spillett are actor/acrobats, and their exuberant athleticism is a joy to watch. The ensemble meanwhile are playing citizens of Old Peking; the challenge here for assistant choreographer Laila Diallo is to plot their moves as they go about their daily business without allowing them to obscure the chase. Before long they find the right flow.

At this point Gareth Valentine, who created the score and is also the musical supervisor, conducts a mini-rehearsal of the show's first moment. He wants the sound of Aladdin's name to be more wraith-like. "I don't want any vibrato, it needs to be as cold as ice," he says. After a couple of attempts, the ensemble finds what he is after.

During the lunch break Sean talks of the difficulties actors have in switching to pantomime mode. "If they get too psychological about it, if there's too much character exploration, the whole fabric dissolves. You have to make a commitment to the material, get on your feet and do it with a very specific attitude and tone. You have to do something very sculpted and clear, in bold colours, and then find out what works and what doesn't. It's no good doing it as if it were a straight play."

He reflects candidly on the difference between this and last year's preparations. "Last Christmas we were really groping in the dark. We had very little technical time to stage what in effect is the equivalent of a big musical. We had to make compromises, which meant we weren't able to get all the sets exactly as he wanted them, and then there was no time to change them. This year we started a week earlier and built in more technical preview time. So we're much more confident."

There have also, he reveals, been significant changes to the script. "Last year we concentrated a lot of energy on the Dame, Abbanazar and Aladdin, all of which bore fruit and was I think very clear. But meanwhile other characters got somewhat neglected. For example, we virtually invented the Hanky and Panky story during rehearsal, whereas this time I think we got the balance for them about right."

There were other characters which seemed to need a rethink. "Dim Sum was underwritten, so we've made adjustments to his character, especially in the opening scene, which we're now exploring with Frances. I think the Emperor – in the revision – was overwritten, so we're now looking for some cuts." The lyrics too have been given a bit of a makeover. "Some of them were written in a hurry, and written for effect rather than for meaning," Sean suggests. "So we've been through everything, and where they are not connected to the story we've cut or rewritten them."

Ian McKellen, delighted to be back as Widow Twankey, muses on the attraction of panto. "It's a form which welcomes anything the theatre can do," he says. "The only restriction is, does it work theatrically?" He also poses a question: "Are the British dotty about theatre because they went to a panto when they were young, or is it that they invented panto because they are so dotty about theatre?"

After lunch the rehearsal resumes, and they take it from the top of the show, with Dim Sum entering on his laundry bicycle. The focus here is on physical detail rather than on character. Which tyre should Dim Sum pump up having been "deflated"? Would a pair of bellows be preferable to a bicycle pump? How can Panky's prodding of the sheet under which Aladdin is hidden be synchronised with Dim Sum's goosing of Hanky?

Throughout the day humour is never far below the surface, with Sean often setting the tone, and the actors entering into the spirit of it. After one unscheduled silence he asks: "Any danger of another line here, or are you all too wrapped up in your own performances?" To Dim Sum, who supposedly hails from Wigan but has suddenly gone all Geordie, he says: "Could we possibly have the same accent that we had yesterday, Miss Barber?" When a group of men in the ensemble appears to have literally lost the plot, he enquires: "Are they members of Equity?" Later there's a huge laugh when Paul, already a confident Emperor with an exquisite sense of timing, does all kinds of unexpected things with his imperial fan.

Considerable time is then spent on the cave scene, where Roger Allam's Abbanazar is soon in full pantomime flight. Relishing the melodrama, he is by turns menacing, suave and monumentally furious. "His anger management isn't terribly good," he comments mildly afterwards. "No, he didn't take his tablets," Sean replies, adding: "That was good, a lot more detail, and new things from last year."

The day ends with Laila spending a couple of hours teaching the ensemble the tricky steps involved in "Pantomime", the big number that closes both acts. They all go at it willingly, and by the end she is satisfied. "It still needs a lot of refinement, but that's a good sketch," she tells them.

Judging by these two very varied sessions, this revival looks set to top the original *Aladdin* production. Sean emphasises the importance of the company's spirit. "If we have fun, the audience has fun. And we're certainly having it now."

A Day Trip to Pantonia

In the lead-up to Christmas 2007, I sat in on an entertaining day of rehearsals for the Old Vic's pantomime Cinderella, *with book and lyrics by Stephen Fry. Director Fiona Laird was putting through their paces a cast that included Sandi Toksvig as the Narrator, Pauline Collins as the Fairy Godmother, and Madeleine Worrall as Cinderella.*

"WE'RE LADY GIRLS, LADY GIRLS / Big and burly lady girls... Move over Moss Bros, forget Diana / It's dishy Dolce and cute Gabbana."

It's ten o'clock in the land of Pantonia, as imagined by Stephen Fry. Decked out in hooped rehearsal skirts, and backed by an all-singing, all-dancing ensemble, the Ugly Sisters (Mark Lockyer and Hal Fowler) are vamping and camping it up to the hilt. Under the watchful and experienced eyes of choreographer Francesca Jaynes and her assistant Dale Mercer, they're running through their number "Lady Girls", offering a wicked range of pouting poses and girlie grimaces as they whirl and twirl between members of the ensemble.

For the principals it's the end of the first week's work in the Jerwood Space rehearsal room (the ensemble have already had a week working on their numbers). Today director Fiona Laird plans to visit again a mixture of straight scenes and song-and-dance numbers. She wants the company to keep in mind that this is not just a pantomime, but a touching rags-to-riches fairy story known by everyone.

After "Lady Girls", the focus switches to Warmleigh House, the home of Cinderella and her wicked stepmother and stepsisters. The sets for the dining room and kitchen, which will be one above the other in the theatre, are here set up side by side by the stage-management team. Stephen Brimson Lewis' ravishing designs for each scene are displayed in computer-generated colour on the back wall of the room, providing a useful point of reference at various moments of the day.

Cinderella (Madeleine Worrall) and her loyal friend Buttons (Paul Keating) are wondering how she can make her sisters' frocks for the ball in such a short time. Fiona helps them block the scene, which involves occasional exchanges between Upstairs and Downstairs via a speaking tube. Paul, now off the book, gets a burst of applause when he runs through his lengthy shopping list of fabrics for the frocks, virtually without hesitation or deviation.

With the help of musical supervisor Neil McArthur on piano, Paul and Madeleine then work on "My Man", their charming fantasy duet ("Oh will we ever see / That very special he"). Both have good, pure voices, and they combine beautifully. There is some discussion as to whether Paul should sing high or low in one key section. Next they have to match the words to their movements. Francesca pushes them to achieve more precision and grace. "Don't bounce, and keep your heels on the floor," she tells Paul. Meanwhile Fiona warns them of the danger of singing to each other in profile. "You must sing with your hearts, but keep looking at each other to a minimum, so we can see your faces."

Next the scene shifts to Upstairs in the dining-room, where the Ugly Sisters and their mother Candida (Debbie Chazen) are getting excited about going to the ball. It's a scene packed with innuendo and sibling rivalry, which they perform with great relish. Fiona asks Debbie to play one of the many double entendres less knowingly: "The more innocent it is, the funnier," she suggests. The tricky section here is the waffles-in-the-face routine: yesterday the actors rehearsed it using foam, but today they're just concentrating on getting the timing right, which they more or less do.

After lunch attention turns to the start of Act 2 and "Not Very Strictly, Come Dancing!", the opening number at the ball. The ensemble attack it with great vigour: the acrobatics are impressive, the overall effect dazzling. Francesca is pleased, but asks for more energy in the links between the different sections of the number. Then, with support from Dale, who offers a valuable second pair of eyes, she works on integrating the principals' movements with those of the chorus.

During a pause Fiona announces that one of the company has had to withdraw from the show because of a dodgy knee. There is sympathy all round among the cast, but also a spate of mock-nervous jokes about the chances for the rest of them surviving the next three weeks' rehearsal ("We're being broken one by one"; "I came already broken," and so on).

Neil McArthur now takes charge. Sitting at the piano, with composer Anne Dudley by his side, he leads the company through the complexities of "If the slipper fits". It's a challenging number in fifteen-part harmony, during which the girls take turns to put on the slipper, and the chorus holds forth on the variety of female shapes and types: "Some girls are thin, some girls are wide / Some girls are blond, some girls are dyed."

It's the first time the principals involved – Sandi Toksvig, Joseph Millson, Debbie Chazen and Penny Laydon – have worked on the song. As they sing, Penny holds a tiny tape recorder in her hand, to enable them to practise their parts later. Neil deals skilfully with individual problems, adjusting a note or a chord where a singer has difficulty with a particular harmony or interval. Once this is sorted out, he positions each of the principals next to a member of the ensemble. As it is throughout, the bawdy pantomime spirit is never far from the surface. Neil: "Sandi, you have backing from the men here." Sandi: "Oh good, it's been years."

While the male ensemble goes off to rehearse elsewhere, Fiona takes Cinderella and the Fairy Godmother (Pauline Collins) through their first encounter. Disguised as "a warty old woman", Pauline quickly shows glimpses of her expert comic timing, and builds up a good rapport with Madeleine, who is proving an appropriately charming yet gutsy Cinderella. Here and there they make tentative suggestions about a move or a position. Fiona, who has a sharp eye for practicalities as well as imaginative flair, readily accepts them. The team spirit is good.

Finally, the three of them work together on the end of Act 1, when the Fairy Godmother explains to Cinderella that she can go to the ball after all. It will be a complicated scene technically, with wires, music, strobe lighting and other effects. Fiona explains in detail how the climax – complete with mice and a surprise magical pumpkin moment – will work, and bring the first half of the show to a conclusion.

And then the clock strikes six, and Cinderella and company disappear into the night.

6

Children's Theatre

Hergé's Adventures of Tintin – Dragon –
Slava's Snowshow – Mr A's Amazing Maze Plays –
Two Weeks with the Queen

Tintin in Tibet

During the winter of 2007-08 Hergé's Adventures of Tintin
played on tour and in London. I caught up with the
acclaimed production in Oxford, and talked to its director
and adapter Rufus Norris about the particular attraction of
this Tintin adventure for a young audience.

THE SHOW IS OVER, BUT the company lingers on. It's
feedback time at the Oxford Playhouse. Having enjoyed a
thrilling matinee performance of *Hergé's Adventures of*
Tintin, a lively group of children from the audience has

gathered eagerly in the front of the stalls, ready to interrogate the actors, who sit in front of them on the edge of the stage.

Many of their questions are about the mechanics of this huge theatrical spectacle, with special reference to the Yeti, aka the Abominable Snowman. Was there a man inside? How was the effect of his footprints achieved? And what about his voice? Other questions focus on how the climbing sequences were done, whether anyone got hurt, why some parts of the story had been missed out, and whether it was difficult to stay in character. All are answered informatively and with good humour.

The show, which has played to great acclaim at the Young Vic and the Barbican, is based on Hergé's book *Tintin in Tibet*, adapted for the stage by director Rufus Norris and playwright David Greig. Vibrant and colourful, hugely imaginative, laced with humour and abounding in energy, the production manages supremely well the tricky task of appealing to children and adults alike.

Tintin the fearless young reporter has of course been a legendary character for decades, and hugely popular internationally. Created in 1929 by Hergé, the pen name for the Belgian artist Georges Remi, the cartoon adventures co-starring Captain Haddock and Snowy the faithful dog are recognised as works of art as well as wonderfully entertaining stories.

After the Young Vic's artistic director David Lan had the idea of staging a Tintin story, he appointed Rufus Norris its director, and gave him an open brief. "As a boy I was more of an Asterix than a Tintin fan," Norris confesses. "But my son read them all when he was five or six, so we had a complete collection. I chose *Tintin in Tibet* because it's the one in which the most happens to Tintin emotionally, and the one with most depth. It also had the most resonance with Hergé: he had a breakdown because of the break-up of his marriage, and wrote the story as a response to it."

The story – Hergé called it "a song of friendship" – concerns Tintin's search for his Chinese friend Chang, whom everyone believes has been killed in a plane crash in the Himalayas. A dream convinces Tintin he is alive but in peril, and with Haddock and Snowy he sets out to test this belief. Along the way they encounter all kinds of obstacles, human as well as physical. Intriguingly, Chang was based on a friend of Hergé, and the story contains a prophecy of what would happen later in their lives.

Another reason for choosing the Tibet story was its relative pictorial simplicity. "In most of the other books Tintin goes all over the place with his adventures," Norris explains. "The colour range is enormous, and would have been a real challenge for the designer. Tibet is a much more controlled palette, mainly white and blue, so it's possible to honour Hergé more faithfully."

The set by Ian Macneil is cleverly constructed to give a sense of the picture-frame elements of the original. The stunning costumes by Joan Wadge are beautifully realised. "We've been very fastidious about them," Norris says. "Obviously we had hundreds of costume drawings at our disposal, and we were lucky to be able to see Hergé's original drawings in Brussels."

He and David Greig have only made slight adjustments to the original story. The book has plenty of humour, much of it emanating from Captain Haddock and the exploits of Snowy, but they've put in a little bit more here and there. They've also added some attractive and varied music, created by Orlando Gough: a torch song in the Swiss Alpine hotel where the story starts; a work song for the Sherpa guides as they climb the mountains; and a chant when Tintin and his friends reach the monastery.

Norris was also attracted to the story because it's not gender specific. "There are no guns, no running around after baddies, it's all about friendship. Tintin isn't a macho character, and neither is he effeminate, so he's accessible to both sexes. I wish there were more women in the story, but the girls in the audience seem as attentive as the boys. Of course there's also the faithful, all-suffering Snowy, who's got enough anarchy in him to misbehave, so everyone loves him."

There's also the giant Yeti, who is initially demonised, but turns out to be a benign character, and one who plays a key role in the story. His presence is probably the reason why the show is recommended for the over-sevens. Yet the four-year-old boy sitting with me had no fear of him, and was clearly entranced throughout this wonderful family show.

All in it Together

The National's family show for 1992 was Dragon *by the Russian writer Yvegeny Shvarts, in a new English version by Alan Cumming and Ultz. I watched an early rehearsal of this uniquely collaborative venture, which involved among many other talents those of MC Kinky and Spitting Image.*

THE SCENE: REHEARSAL ROOM 2 at the National Theatre. The time: Friday morning, six weeks before opening night. Two tightly bunched groups of actors move around the large, bare space, first menacingly, then fearfully, then seductively. The movement teacher walks between and around them, encouraging, helping, criticising. "You've got to learn how to think and move together," she says.

It's the fifth day of rehearsal for the cast of *Dragon*, and a tiring one. Already they have been moving around the room like flocks of birds, groups of lizards and herds of antelope. They're concentrating on working as a chorus, so have modelled themselves on anything in nature that moves in a bunch. They have to learn how to depend on each other, but still be able to react spontaneously and inventively.

Dragon has had a chequered history. Combining elements of Russian folklore with stinging satire, it was written and performed in 1943 in the middle of Stalin's tyrannical rule. It was banned after its first performance and not staged again until the mid-1960s – by which time its author was dead.

The play is supposedly set in a small town in Scandinavia at the beginning of the last century. At one level it operates as a humorous, all-action entertainment for children, with the traditional ingredients of dragons, villains, maidens in distress and a heroic knight – who is even called Lancelot. But it also works as a full-blooded political satire, of a society so bowed down by tyranny that, as one character puts it, "Even the ashtrays do what they're told."

Working as a team, but allowing individuals a chance to display their talents, is the essential philosophy of the National's production. This is reflected in the decision by Ultz, the director and designer, to "double-cast" the main parts, giving everyone a chance to play a decent role. "I think if there were two or three major stars and the rest of the actors were just plain bit parts it would be an unhappy show to perform," he says. "But when you have everyone motoring different bits on different nights, the group responsibility keeps it alive. Besides, I think having a two-tier company would be wrong for a play that looks at what that kind of division can do in a particular community."

Dragon was chosen for performance at the National for a number of reasons. It was originally recommended a couple of years ago by literary manager Giles Croft. Jenny Harris, the head of education, was undertaking research into the potential for using puppetry with live performers, and saw that *Dragon* would be a perfect vehicle. Sonia Friedman, the education manager, realised that the project would also continue the tradition of creating family shows such as *Hiawatha*, *The Pied Piper* and *Whale*. At the same time Richard Eyre, the artistic director, had been wanting to work with Spitting Image, and was also discussing various projects with Ultz. *Dragon* seemed to fit the bill for all concerned.

Unusually for a National production, some of the actors have the chance to contribute to the script. Although the translation, by Alan Cumming and Ultz, is in typed form at this stage, Ultz is keen to make use of the talents of his cast – especially when it includes certain street entertainers and stand-up comics, who know a thing or two about improvisation.

So today, as Mark Heap and Mark Saban (Burgomaster Double Act) rehearse with Paul Medford (Henrik) a scene where the dragon flies over their heads, Ultz encourages the two Marks to play around with the situation, to try out some gags of their own. The actors go for it, clearly loving the chance to experiment. On the floor a tape machine records their words, so that anything that works well can be woven into the script later.

Even then there will be scope for improvisation on the

night – but not just in the script. The gypsy band, for instance, are not confined to a set musical score. "We want to leave certain things to chance," says musical director Neil McArthur. "We'll be improvising a lot, although it will have to be within certain limits."

Right now he's gearing up for a meeting with the show's music composer, MC Kinky. The young rap singer/song-writer is an unusual choice for the job. While she's toured with Boy George and written dance music, she's never worked in a theatre before, let alone the National. Although she's white, Ultz felt her kind of "black" sound was spot-on for the alternative, anarchic lifestyle of the gypsy band.

She herself seems very relaxed about the whole project. "Yes, it's very different from doing records," she says. "When you work on a single, you have to think about what's current and what's going to sell. With this, it's just going on the total vibe of the show. I can do what I want musically, although I'm anchored down a bit."

She says her brief from Ultz is "to do what you do". She's about to get together with Neil McArthur in the studio, to work on the gypsy songs, and on various sound effects. "I'll come up with some acidy samples and techno bits and pieces, and then we'll work on the reggae stuff," she says. "But if the music's not working in rehearsal and someone wants it changed, I'll change it. I don't care; I'm not precious."

Making sure the music is right is just one of the responsibilities of the director. Another crucial one is to work closely with the designer. This has proved easier than usual, since Ultz – an experienced designer, with *Arturo Ui* at the National and the RSC's *The Thebans* among his recent credits – is tackling both jobs himself.

For Irene Bohan, the costume supervisor, this has been a

great advantage. "You're near the seat of power this way," she says. "Normally you're doing a costume fitting and thinking, 'Help, is the director going to like this?' With this show he's here on the spot, and you can make immediate design decisions as you go along. That's wonderful."

While some designers simply require her to organise the costumes, Ultz has encouraged her to make suggestions. "That's great, it makes life much more interesting," she says. Together they've looked at Scandinavian costume books, collections of illustrated fairy tales, and other sources. Ultz draws quick sketches as they talk, to help develop his ideas.

For the gypsy band, Irene's costume research has been different from usual. She and her assistant have been round the shops and the street, finding out what young people are wearing. "It's more difficult than historical research, because it's changing all the time," she says. "If we were going to put the gypsies in trainers, they'd have to be the right ones exactly, because there will be kids in the audience saying, 'Oh those went out of fashion weeks ago.' "

Like other National staff working on *Dragon*, her job has been made more complicated by the puppets. But it's also meant more of a challenge: what other show would require the costume department to come up with a jacket with six-foot arms, or decide how a parrot should best be dressed?

Teamwork has also been essential with the creation of the puppets, especially since the making of them, for reasons of time, money and expertise, has been shared between the National's props workshop and Spitting Image. For the Burgomaster, for instance, Spitting Image has done the design and working drawings, but produced the wobbly arms jointly with the National staff.

Like MC Kinky, Spitting Image has not done theatre work before. Its director Roger Law says: "It's very different from television: you've got to solve the problem of how things will work night after night." For Ultz it was an obvious choice: "We went to Spitting Image because they're the greatest experimenters in modern puppet work in this country. Some of their puppets will probably seem more alive than the humans – but that's what the play is about, how people can be robotised."

Again, the crucial early design work was done co-operatively. Prompted by Ultz, puppet-maker Scott Brooker from Spitting Image dug around for visual inspiration in some very offbeat sources: the early German satirical magazine *Simplicissimus*; books showing the half-human, half-animal drawings of the Victorian illustrator Grandville; and examples of Soviet propaganda art from the Stalinist period.

"Once we communicated visually, we really started," Scott recalls. He produced a set of working drawings for the "puppety" characters, coming up with solutions to some of the tricky technical problems – such as how to hide the puppeteer under the blue cat, or make sure the Burgomaster stayed upright inside his huge, inflatable body.

Dragon is a show that is clearly stimulating all kinds of people to be highly creative. As with any production, there's a thing called the budget, and keeping within it can be a real problem. The Olivier, for instance, is one of the biggest stages in the country: just to put a flat floor down can cost £8,000, while buying a cyclorama will leave you little change out of £4,000. "It's always a battle with the figures," admits production manager Annie Gosney, who holds the purse strings.

For *Dragon* she has had continual discussions with Ultz about the set, from outline design onwards. While allowing his ideas to flow, her job has been to remind him what is practical, workable and affordable. "Things always get whittled down and simplified," she explains. "There's always one aspect that's unworkable, whether because of size or cost, or for artistic reasons."

There are other challenges too. Because *Dragon* has morning, afternoon and evening performances, and is in the Olivier repertoire with *Pygmalion* and *Square Rounds*, the crew has to be able to put up and take down the set in fifty minutes on each occasion, instead of the normal four hours. "It's very demanding, it calls for everyone's ingenuity," Annie says.

Despite all the problems, the *Dragon* team obviously relish working on a show where things are left open or fluid longer than usual, and where the director has encouraged a more collaborative way of working. Ultz has tried to create a temporary mini-ensemble. It's refreshing that you can do this at the National.

That's Snow Business!

In the autumn of 2006 I had the good fortune to watch the famous Russian clown Slava in action during his latest UK tour of his celebrated Snowshow, *and to talk afterwards with this remarkable man, whom many people consider a genius.*

SLAVA POINTS AT THE CHILDREN playing with the artificial snow in front of us. "I was as young as they are when I first wanted to be a clown. But I didn't make the choice myself, it was chosen for me. It could have been my mother, it could have been God. I don't know which it was. It just happened, and I couldn't resist it."

We're sitting in a corner of the stalls of the spacious Milton Keynes Theatre, where this internationally acclaimed Russian clown has been entrancing a vast audience of all ages with his *Snowshow*. Since it ended twenty minutes ago children have been crowding around him, scooping up handfuls of "snow" from the floor of the auditorium, and pouring them gleefully over his head. A small, seemingly vulnerable figure, dressed in a baggy yellow suit, with a red nose and straggly greying hair, he sits there without moving, passively accepting these heartfelt tributes.

His *Snowshow* contains many ingredients, from the small-scale to the gigantic. There are intimate, subtly executed mime sketches, in which Slava and his troupe of clowns mix humour with pain, and moments of hilarity with surrealist images. At the other end of the scale are the spectacular, visually stunning special effects, involving light, sound, water, cobwebs, balloons, and of course snow, not to mention unexpected moments of audience participation.

This is the first night of the show's nine-week UK tour, and Milton Keynes clearly loves it. But Slava, who likes to call his performances "work in progress", points out through his Russian interpreter that this is just the start: 'It's touching the ground at the moment, just tiptoeing quietly. It's not flying yet, but it will quickly adjust. In two or three days it will be different."

Slava's work is known throughout the world. Now 56, he has played in some eighty cities, and won a clutch of awards, including a Stanislavsky Award in Moscow, a Golden Nose Prize in Barcelona, and a Drama Desk Award in New York. He has brought his show to the UK half a dozen times before, winning a Time Out Award in 1994, and an Olivier Award for Best Entertainment in 1998.

Many people have called him a genius; he describes himself as both an anarchist and an existentialist. When I ask him to explain these labels further, he avoids doing so directly, but says: "Clowns have a lot of faces, and anarchist is just one of them. Existentialist is another one. He is also a poet, a madman, a doctor, and a child. There is a lot of substance to a clown."

His own appeal on stage relies on a potent mixture of the poet and the child. His persona is that of a quizzical, vulnerable human being, shuffling around in a bleak, anonymous, Beckettian landscape: not for nothing was his first show called *Waiting for Dodo*. Often he is the victim of events, but at other times the instigator of them, mixing it with the other clowns with their bizarre hats and Little Tich boots, and in between creating a series of beautiful, elemental images with a variety of props.

He was born Slava Polunin in a village in Russia, where the surrounding fields, forest and river became his playground. It was a childhood built on fantasy: lacking any toys, he invented his own, and as he grew older he invented stories, built tree houses, and created whole towns out of snow. At 17 he went to Leningrad to study engineering, but ended up in a mime studio, where he learned the art of clowning. In 1979 he founded his own theatre company, members of which later moved on to form their own companies, or to appear in productions by Cirque du Soleil.

His own influences and heroes are legion. "If I wanted to write all their names on my wall at home, I wouldn't have enough room," he says. "I like so many, whether they come from the ballet, from art, or from the cinema." He has a particular fondness for the famous figures of the silent-film era: at his home in France he has a large collection of

DVDs of their films, and has watched all those featuring Charlie Chaplin and Buster Keaton. "Keaton I feel very close to, because he is a philosopher. But my favourite is Harry Langdon, because he is very gentle."

As a few children near us continue to play with the snow, I ask him about the climactic moment of the show, which compels the audience to remain long after it has formally ended. "It's impossible to explain its magic, but it always works," he says. "I feel it has to be there. After the tragic moment they have just lived through they need hope, and that's what it provides."

Sounds Peculiar

In Mr A's Amazing Maze Plays *Alan Ayckbourn reveals his abiding love of technology. In the spring of 1993 I watched him in playful mood, directing a work that he described as "written for children and intelligent adults".*

WHEN IS A CHICKEN NOT a chicken? – When it's a bedspring. At least that's what Suzy and Neville discover when they explore Mr Accousticus' weird and wonderful house. That and a lot more besides, for nothing in Mr A's house sounds quite as it should do: a bat shrieks like a car horn, a trapdoor moos like a cow, an alarm clock quacks...

Mr A's Amazing Maze Plays is not Ayckbourn's first play in which sound plays such an important part. One of his plays for adults, *Henceforward...*, is all about a man who puts microphones in every room in his house, so that he can use recordings of his family's voices to help him create his music. So it comes as no surprise to find that Britain's most successful playwright is something of a technology freak. Back at his home in Scarborough he has a mass of sound equipment and a library of special effects that would probably make Mr Accousticus go green with envy.

So how did this interest in technology begin? "I've been fascinated by sounds ever since I was a child," says the real-life Mr A. "At the time I was given a portable Grundig reel-to-reel tape recorder – it now seems like it weighed three tons. I used to play around with it a lot, record speeches for myself, and write radio plays which I would act out in odd locations."

Later, as a young man, he became a radio drama producer for the BBC, at a time when they were just beginning to use tape on location. "I suppose I was one of the first radio producers to do that," he says. "It was like editing film, but without all the expense."

These days he runs the Stephen Joseph Theatre in Scarborough on the North Yorkshire coast, where nearly all his plays have their first showing. This gives him plenty of opportunity to try out all kinds of technical experiments, both in the theatre and at home. Recently he's become fascinated by digital sampling, which is what the sound effects for the National's production are based on.

As normally happens with his plays, Ayckbourn is directing the National production himself. You don't need to spend long watching a rehearsal to catch his delight in experimenting with the possible uses of sound: many of the effects used bring forth heavy chuckles from him.

"Alan can do this as well as I can," says Freya Edwards, the National's sound technician for the production. She's sitting by her sampler and keyboard on the edge of the large playing space of the Mermaid Theatre, where early rehearsals are being held. The equipment is covered in sheets of paper on which are written her notes for the sound cues, such as "Owl – C3 – Hoot (Slow/Long)" or

"Cat – E3 – Yowl/Hiss/Meow".

Over on the set the play's author/director, decked out in colour-splashed T-shirt and trainers, is working with Suzy (Judith McSpadden) and Neville (Adam Godley) to match the right (or the wrong) sound to their movements, as they scramble, creep and climb through Mr Accousticus' many rooms.

"Do you want one lot of chickens or two?" Freya asks. This is her first day actually in rehearsal. She has spent the previous two weeks putting together the sounds already mentioned in the script – the second part of the play calls for some seventy sound effects, thirty of them in Mr Accousticus' Cabinet of Sounds.

But she's also built up, on a second sampler, a library of extra sounds for possible use. "If Alan wants to hear a bang or a squeak or a pop, I can insert it into the main sampler, and he can hear it instantly," she explains. "But it must be something that the audience will recognise straight away." To get the sounds she may use her own voice, and then "stretch" it, or change the pitch. She takes some of the musical-instrument sounds off CDs, but to get something new and different she likes to wander into the National's prop store, and make sounds with a great variety of objects.

Ayckbourn is impressed with the results. "It's very much the way we work with digital sampling in Scarborough," he says. "I think of Freya as the ninth member of the cast." Already he has asked for half a dozen sounds that aren't in the script. "It's enjoyable but a bit hair-raising," Freya says. "Anything could happen."

Just now Suzy and Neville are about to creep into yet another room, and the director decides he needs a "wrong" sound for the door opening. "How about a donkey?" Freya suggests. "Mmm," he says, and rolls the idea around his tongue: "Eee-yore, Eee-yore. Yes, let's have a donkey." And he gives another chuckle.

Ayckbourn says he wrote the play because he liked the idea of a man who steals sound in order to create silence. Of course the play also offers wonderful possibilities for words to be put in different people's mouths – which is also what playwriting is about. But he also hopes the play will sell the idea of live theatre to younger audiences, especially since in *Mr A's Amazing Maze Plays* they are involved in decisions about telling the story. "I think the last year or so young people have been turning back to theatre, as if they'd had enough of special effects in films and videos," he says. "Once you've seen one head swivel or explode there's nowhere else to go."

But isn't there a possibility in stories such as this one, with its variety of technical tricks, that the real-life characters might take second place to all those effects created by digital samplers and sound mics? Yes, he says, he is aware of the danger. "Sounds are very important, but you can easily fall into the trap of getting all the effects you want, while missing out on the important things. It's vital that the technical magic doesn't get in the way of the human magic."

Seriously Funny

Two Weeks with the Queen *is an Australian play by Mary Morris, adapted from the novel by Morris Gleitzman. In 1994 Richard Eyre, then director of the National Theatre, explained to me why he was bringing this comic play into the repertoire.*

RICHARD EYRE HAS STRONG FEELINGS about children's theatre. "We've woefully neglected it in this country, so it's become a kind of ghetto," he says. It's this kind of conviction that has led him to agree to stage a highly original new play, which somehow manages to be hilariously funny while dealing with very serious issues.

Two Weeks with the Queen is the story of twelve-year-old Colin, whose brother is dying. In his desire to help he writes a letter to Buckingham Palace:

Dear Your Majesty the Queen

I need to speak to you urgently about my brother Luke. He's got cancer, and the doctors in Australia are being really slack. If I could borrow your doctor for a few days I know he/she would fix things up in no time. Of course Mum and Dad would pay his/her fares, even if it meant selling the car or getting a loan. Please contact me at the above address urgently.

Yours sincerely, Colin Mudford

PS This is not a hoax. Ring the above number and Auntie Iris will tell you.

The action of the play is fuelled by Colin's unbounded energy, optimism, and determination to surmount every obstacle that the adults keep putting in his way. During his fortnight in "Tommy Land" he gets in all sorts of trouble, but continually outwits his dreary suburban aunt and uncle with whom he's staying. He also teaches a thing or two to his down-trodden cousin Alastair, whom he befriends.

Two Weeks with the Queen deals with issues such as terminal illness, AIDS, homosexuality, and children's rights. Yet its hilarious dialogue, and Colin's unflagging exuberance and resilience, make it highly entertaining even while it subtly explores ideas about friendship, plain dealing, and the parental oppression of children.

The play has been hugely successful in Australia, where

it was staged by Wayne Harrison, artistic director of the Sydney Theatre Company, and where Alastair has become a national hero for the way he finally shakes off the parental yoke. In London, as a co-production between the Stephen Joseph Theatre in Scarborough and the National, it will be directed by Alan Ayckbourn, who is keen to break down the barriers between young people's theatre and adult theatre.

So too is Richard Eyre, who believes the play is wonderfully funny and very original. "When I first came across it, I felt the same as I did with *Angels in America* – this is good! It's very difficult to find writing for children that isn't patronising, twee or just obnoxious. But I don't see why children should get stuck with second-rate work."

7

Playwrights

Federico García Lorca – Philip Barry –
Tennessee Williams – Oscar Wilde

Federico García Lorca: The Poetic Revolutionary

As the National prepared in 2000 to stage David Hare's new version of Lorca's last play The House of Bernarda Alba, *I put together a brief guide to the great Spanish playwright's life and work.*

LORCA HAS BECOME ALMOST AS famous for his death as for his work. In the early days of the Spanish Civil War in 1936, only two months after completing *The House of Bernarda Alba*, a play he was never to see staged, he was arrested by the fascists, taken out into an olive grove near Granada, and shot by Franco's paramilitary Black Squad. He was 38.

Nearly sixty years on his body has still not been identified.

Now acknowledged as the greatest Spanish playwright of the twentieth century, Lorca was initially celebrated as a poet, most notably for his Gypsy Ballads. In his early plays – two Surrealist ones were inspired by his friendship with Salvador Dalì and Luis Buñuel – he experimented with different forms, including farce, puppetry and historical verse drama, but without great success.

In 1931 he formed his own student theatre company, La Barraca, which with government funding gave free performances of classic plays to rural audiences throughout Spain. This experience enabled Lorca to add directing, stage managing, training actors and adapting plays to his skills as a poet, musician and painter.

His status as a major playwright is based on his last three works, *Blood Wedding, Yerma* and *The House of Bernarda Alba*. Though often described as a trilogy, only the first two plays were part of his planned "trilogy of the Spanish earth". Nevertheless the three plays have several themes in common: set in the Andalusian countryside of Lorca's youth, they explore the hard nature of rural life, the oppression of women in a male-dominated society, and the conflict between love and honour, between desire and repression. All three plays end with a violent death.

The works were revolutionary in the way Lorca used poetry and prose within the same play. This is most marked in *Blood Wedding*, where he confidently and skilfully uses poetry and song to move the action forward, creating in the violent third act several sections of mysterious, beautiful and sensuous poetry. There is much less verse in *Yerma*, and hardly any at all in *Bernarda Alba*. Yet perhaps because Lorca's prose is inherently poetic, the two forms seem to flow easily into each other.

Blood Wedding was based on a story Lorca had read in a newspaper, about a bride eloping with her cousin on her wedding day. It mixes realistic scenes between the feuding families with increasing symbolism in the later scenes, in which a group of woodcutters act as a Greek-style Chorus, and the Moon and Death appear as characters. The play, premiered in 1933 under Lorca's own direction, was acclaimed for returning tragic poetry to the Spanish theatre.

Yerma, on the other hand, was savagely criticised when it was staged in Madrid the following year, the right-wing press declaring it to be an attack on decency and traditional Spanish values. The story of a woman whose husband refuses to give her a child was certainly a subversive one, exposing as it did the injustice of the Spanish male's traditional right to demand absolute obedience from his wife.

Lorca described *The House of Bernarda Alba* as "a photographic documentary". On the face of it the story is simply a family drama centering on the repressive widow and matriarch Bernarda, whose refusal to let her five daughters have any emotional life has tragic consequences. Yet Lorca clearly intended the play to have a wider meaning: already a socialist and an active supporter of the Popular Front, he was now declaring himself an "enthusiastic, devoted follower of the theatre of social action".

So in *Bernarda Alba* he deliberately wrote less poetically, in order that his targets would be more discernible. His attack is on the relentless power of money, on the way personal freedom is curtailed by repressive rules and regulations, and on the desire to preserve outward appearances at the expense of human emotions. In a strict Catholic society about to be taken over by a fascist regime, these themes were not welcomed – as Lorca was soon tragically to discover for himself.

Philip Barry: The Satirical Insider

To accompany my programme piece about the Old Vic's 2005 production of Philip Barry's The Philadelphia Story, *I wrote a brief account of his life and work, and the play's origins and success on Broadway.*

LABELLED "THE GENTLEMAN PLAYWRIGHT", and compared in his day to Noël Coward, Philip Barry was one of the leading American playwrights of the 1920s and 1930s. Yet he wasn't merely a writer of sparkling comedies reflecting the rituals of the idle rich; he also wrote serious, experimental plays, religious allegories and political dramas which explored class conflict, totalitarianism and Freudian psychology, and showed a darker side to his personality.

Among them were allegorical works such as *Hotel Universe* and *Here Come the Clowns*, full of mystical and symbolic overtones, and *John*, a drama about John the Baptist. These plays generally had short runs, attracted hostile reviews, and baffled American audiences, who preferred his comedies of manners satirising high society, such as *Paris Bound* and *Holiday*. *The Philadelphia Story* was the most successful of his twenty plays and, with its crackling wit, and romantic stories set in a world he knew from the inside, it's been the one that has lasted.

Born in 1896 in Rochester, New York, to middle-class parents of Irish descent, Barry started writing at the age of nine. Educated at Yale, he enrolled on the famous English 47 Workshop at Harvard University directed by George Pierce Baker, who helped to launch the careers of Eugene

O'Neill, George Abbott and S. N. Bellman. Rejected by the army because of poor eyesight when America entered the war, he worked in London in the code department of the US embassy. In 1922 he married his childhood sweetheart Ellen Semple, the daughter of a wealthy lawyer, who gave the couple a house in New York and a villa in Cannes, where they became friends with Hemingway, Fitzgerald and other Riviera literati.

Barry was fascinated by the aura of exclusivity that surrounded the privileged, cocktail-drinking classes, and spent as much time as he could among them. He always displayed impeccable taste, wearing the best hand-tailored clothes, and speaking with a distinctly Ivy League drawl. He was, one critic complained, "too partial to good society". Yet it was his familiarity and sympathy with those who belonged to it that enabled him to portray them with satirical accuracy and wry affection.

The Philadelphia Story came at an opportune moment in his career, for his previous three plays had failed. His initial idea was for a story about a wealthy family who were to be the subject of an article in *Fortune* magazine. His wife suggested he set it in the fashionable Main Line area of Philadelphia, where, in contrast to New York and Chicago, "old" money and "old" families counted for everything. He based his main character in part on Hope Montgomery Scott, a racy, sporty and wealthy socialite belonging to an "ancient" Philadelphia family.

Married when young to Edgar Scott, the heir to the Pennsylvania Railroad fortune, she was considered one of the best-dressed women of the age. Her beauty and slim, angular figure attracted the attention of artists: Cecil Beaton took several portraits, while Augustus John painted her twice. She mingled with the famous, doing the Charleston with Josephine Baker in Paris, a foxtrot with the Duke of Windsor, and lunch with Winston Churchill. At their house on the 750-acre Montgomery Estate the Scotts entertained lavishly, with grand dinner parties and dances. Barry was a classmate of Edgar Scott, so was able to observe his model from close quarters.

In the summer of 1938 he took his idea to Katharine Hepburn, who had just played the society-girl heroine in the film version of his play *Holiday*. Hepburn's career was at a critical point: her last six films, including *Bringing Up Baby* and *Holiday*, had not been commercial successes, and she had recently appeared at the top of a list of stars who were deemed "box-office poison" (she was, however, in good company: the list included Fred Astaire, Joan Crawford, Marlene Dietrich and Greta Garbo). Her first love was the theatre, but her career wasn't flourishing: the critics had persistently attacked her for being affected and remote on stage. Dorothy Parker had famously remarked that "she ran the gamut of emotion from A to B", while the critic Brooks Atkinson had written of "a voice that has an unpleasant timbre".

Barry's story appealed to Hepburn, and she immediately encouraged him to develop it further. As they discussed the script, its focus shifted onto the priggish, "ice-goddess" heroine. There were many parallels between Barry's heroine and Hepburn: their fierce independence and pride, their hatred of the press, their love of swimming, and their concern for the family name. Now Barry consciously shaped the part as a vehicle for Hepburn, for her wit and intelligence, her striking voice and features.

The Theatre Guild offered to produce it, but was only able to put up half the money. Howard Hughes, Hepburn's erstwhile lover and now friend (he still let her fly his plane), agreed to provide the other half jointly with Hepburn. Once she knew she had failed to secure the part of Scarlett O'Hara in *Gone with the Wind*, Hepburn and the play went into rehearsal. But she and director Robert Sinclair were unhappy with the third act, so Barry rewrote it, giving less emphasis to the hostility between Tracy Lord and her philandering father, with which Hepburn apparently felt uncomfortable.

After successful try-out weeks in New Haven, Philadelphia and Washington DC in the spring of 1939, a decision had to be made whether to take the production straight in to New York. Everyone but Hepburn felt they should risk it: "Do anything you want, throw your money away," she is supposed to have said in despair. Terrified of New York and the critics, four hours before the opening at the Shubert Theatre she locked herself in her room at the Waldorf-Astoria, repeating the words "This is Indianapolis! This is Indianapolis!" to try to persuade herself she was still on tour.

She needn't have worried. With Van Heflin playing Macaulay Connor, Joseph Cotten as C. K. Dexter Haven, and Shirley Booth as Liz Imbrie, she scored a full-blooded triumph, and finally won over the critics. Brooks Atkinson felt she played Tracy "like a woman who has at last found the joy she has always been seeking in the theatre", while John Mason Brown wrote: "The radiant Miss Hepburn brings a loveliness to our stage such as has not been seen hereabouts in years." The play ran for 415 performances.

Meanwhile, at Howard Hughes' prompting, Hepburn had cannily bought the film rights. She quickly sold them to MGM, securing choice of director (she chose George Cukor), but not of cast. She wanted Spencer Tracy, whom she hadn't yet met, as C. K. Dexter Haven, and Clark Gable as Macaulay Connor, but had to "settle" for Cary Grant and James Stewart. Barry, presumably to his regret, asked for too much money to write the screenplay, and the job went to Donald Ogden Stewart.

Grant insisted on, and got, top billing, but the film, shot while Hepburn was still playing the part on stage, undoubtedly belongs to her. The critic of *Life* wrote: "When Katharine Hepburn sets out to play Katharine Hepburn she is a sight to behold. No one is then her equal." The rest is film history, and a lasting monument to the impish wit and wisdom of Philip Barry.

Tennessee Williams: Timeless Themes

While a National company headed by Zoë Wanamaker were rehearsing The Rose Tattoo *in 2007, I wrote a brief summary of Tennessee Williams' life and work, and of the stage history of the play.*

THOMAS LANIER WILLIAMS WAS BORN in March 1911 in the small Southern town of Columbus, Mississippi, in the home of his maternal grandfather, the local Episcopal rector. His father, Cornelius Williams, a coarse, violent man, a drunkard and a womaniser, was a travelling shoe salesman, who spent much of the time away from his family. His mother, Edwina Dakin, was a high-minded, prudish and socially ambitious woman, who put great emphasis on correct Southern manners and etiquette.

His sheltered childhood ended when the family moved in 1918 to the city of St Louis, Missouri. His father called him "Miss Nancy", because he preferred reading books to playing baseball. He started writing poetry and stories at 14 to escape the misery of his home life. He was very close to his older sister Rose, who was mentally unstable, eventually diagnosed as schizophrenic, and institutionalised. Later, without her brother knowing, her parents agreed to her undergoing a pre-frontal lobotomy, an event which had a profound impact on the playwright's life and works.

In 1929 he entered the University of Missouri at Columbia, where he started to write plays, and was nicknamed "Tennessee" by his fellow-students, because of his southern drawl. In 1932 his father, who worked for the International Shoe Company, withdrew him from the university before he could complete his degree, and secured him a job as a temporary office clerk in the firm's warehouse, where he worked for a year.

In 1935, with financial help from his grandparents, he attended Washington University in St Louis. Two years later he moved to Iowa State University to study playwriting, and on leaving there the following year to go to New Orleans, he formally adopted "Tennessee" as his writing name. In order to survive he took several odd jobs, including those of waiter, lift operator and cinema usher. In 1939 he was awarded a Theatre Guild prize of $100 for four one-act plays entitled *American Blues*. The following year he received a $1,000 writing fellowship from the Dramatists' Guild. This enabled him to write his first full-length play, *Battle of Angels*, which was staged in Boston by the Theatre Guild, but failed to make it to Broadway (he later rewrote it as *Orpheus Descending*).

Ineligible to serve in the second world war because of a heart condition, he was employed as a screenwriter by MGM, but never took to the work. He subsequently lived in great poverty until his first success on Broadway in 1944, *The Glass Menagerie*, starring Laurette Taylor. While living in New Orleans he wrote *A Streetcar Named Desire*, staged in 1947 with Jessica Tandy and Marlon Brando. The play won three major awards, including the Pulitzer Prize. A year later he wrote *Summer and Smoke*, and then began the main long-term relationship of his life with Frank Merlo, a 25-year-old second-generation Sicilian.

Unable to write openly about his homosexuality, he had his most fertile period in the 1950s, a decade marked by the publication of his novel *The Roman Spring of Mrs Stone*, the film of *Baby Doll*, and the first productions in New York of *The Rose Tattoo, Camino Real, Cat on a Hot Tin Roof, Orpheus Descending, Suddenly Last Summer* and *Sweet Bird of Youth*. After *Period of Adjustment* and *The Night of the Iguana* his popularity declined: his later, more experimental works were neither a commercial nor an artistic success.

He spent many of his later years in ill-health, travelling incessantly in Europe, his life becoming increasingly fuelled by alcohol and drugs. After Frank Merlo died of lung cancer in 1962, he went into a deep depression that lasted for ten years – he called it his "Stoned Age". In 1969 he suffered a nervous breakdown; in 1975 he published his *Memoirs*. His last play to be staged in New York was *Something Cloudy, Something Clear* in 1981. Two years later, in his residence at the Hotel Elysée in New York, he choked to death on the cap of a bottle of pills. He was buried in St Louis.

Tennessee Williams was a prolific writer. In addition to twenty-five full length plays, he produced more than forty short plays, a dozen screenplays, an opera libretto, two novels, a novella, more than sixty short stories, over one hundred poems, an autobiography, a volume of letters, several introductions to plays and books by other writers, and occasional articles and reviews. His works have been translated into more than twenty-seven languages, and countless productions of his work have been staged around the world.

Between 1945 and 1960 he was the most popular playwright in America. He was hailed as an original lyrical voice in the American theatre, a brilliant creator of theatrical atmosphere, who provided spectacular and bravura acting parts. His controversial plays, drawing heavily on his own troubled and chaotic life, dealt in a poetic manner with repressed sexuality and family conflict. As he himself said: "Everything a writer produces is his inner history, transposed into another time."

His themes were timeless and intensely personal: he wrote about illusion and deceit, the fear of madness, violence and tenderness, the battle between repression and release, despair and hope, corruption and betrayal, the pain and pleasure of sex, the redemptive power of love, and the destructive nature of time. His fragile, sensitive and generally sympathetic characters are often outsiders or among the dispossessed, gallantly battling against their circumstances.

The Rose Tattoo is set on the Gulf Coast of America between New Orleans and Mobile, in a small village populated mostly by Sicilian-American families. It tells the story of the passionate and devout widow Serafina Delle Rose. Williams' intense feelings about his damaged sister Rose are reflected in the central imagery: Serafina's daughter is Rosa, her husband is Rosario, and both she and her two men sport a rose tattoo at different times. Rosa, like her real-life counterpart, "had a very strict mother and wasn't allowed to go on dates with boys". But there are also other, more classical allusions, for example to the mystic rose of religious literature, and the rose window of the medieval cathedral.

Williams described the play as one that depicted "the Dionysian element in human life," that contained "the lyric as well as the Bacchantic impulse"; it was, he wrote, "a celebration of the inebriate god". It was first performed in Chicago at the Erlinger in December 1950, produced by Cheryl Crawford and directed by Daniel Mann. The part of Serafina was written with Anna Magnani in mind, but the Italian film actress was worried about her command of English, and declined to play it on stage, preferring to wait for the film version. The role was taken by Maureen Stapleton, with Eli Wallach playing Alvaro Mangiacavallo.

Following various criticisms, Williams made many changes, so that for several performances in Chicago the play was performed with a different ending each night. It opened on Broadway in February 1951 at the Martin Beck, and was an instant success. Its two stars won Tony awards, as did the play and the designer. When the play was presented at the first Dublin Festival in 1957, its treatment of illicit love resulted in it being closed down by the police, the arrest of the festival's founder, and the cancellation of the following year's festival.

The Rose Tattoo had its UK premiere at the New Shakespeare in Liverpool in December 1958, with Sam Wanamaker both directing and playing Alvaro, and Lea Padovani cast as Serafina. The production opened in London in February 1959 at the New, with Bill Nagy taking over as Alvaro. The film version was released in 1955, directed by Daniel Mann: Anna Magnani played Serafina opposite Burt Lancaster as Alvaro Mangiacavallo, and won the Oscar for Best Actress.

Oscar Wilde: Sense and Nonsense

In the programme for Peter Gill's 2008 production of The Importance of Being Earnest *in the West End, starring Penelope Keith as Lady Bracknell, I contributed a piece about Oscar Wilde's eventful and ultimately tragic life, and the themes of his major plays.*

OSCAR FINGALLS O'FLAHERTIE WILLS WILDE was born in Dublin on 15 October 1856, the son of William Wilde, an eye and ear surgeon, and Jane Wilde, an Irish nationalist poetess writing as "Speranza". He was educated at Port Royal School in Enniskillen; at Trinity College, Dublin, where he won the Berkeley Medal for Greek; and at Magdalen College, Oxford, where he won the Newdigate Prize for English Verse. A self-confessed aesthete, he was known at Oxford for his generosity, wit and good nature, although his effeminate behaviour provoked a group of undergraduates to wreck his rooms and duck him in the river Cherwell.

After Oxford he settled in London, where his brilliant conversation, unconventional dress, long hair and iconoclastic views made him all the rage in society; he was also lampooned in *Punch*, and satirised as Bunthorne in Gilbert and Sullivan's *Patience*. In 1882 he embarked on a hugely successful tour of the USA and Canada, lecturing on art, poetry and house decoration. Two years later he married Constance Lloyd, the daughter of a wealthy Dublin barrister; they lived in Chelsea and had two sons. He contributed to literary and artistic journals, was editor for two years of the magazine *Woman's World*, and finally achieved prominence as a writer in the 1890s, first with his novel *The Picture of Dorian Grey*, and then with his plays.

In 1892 he fell in love with Lord Alfred Douglas, provoking Lord Queensberry, Douglas' father, to accuse Wilde of "posing as a sodomite". Wilde sued him for criminal libel, lost the case, and was himself prosecuted. Found guilty of homosexual offences, he was sentenced to two years' imprisonment with hard labour. In prison he wrote *The Ballad of Reading Gaol*, and a letter to Douglas, later published as *De Profundis*. After his release he left England for ever. He lived in France and, in 1900, penniless, died of meningitis in Paris, having been received into the Catholic Church.

Wilde's continuing fame and popularity as a dramatist more than a century after his death is based on four major plays, originally staged in London during the 1890s. The first, *Lady Windermere's Fan*, established him as a playwright; the last, *The Importance of Being Earnest*, has been described as the greatest comedy ever written. These comedies of manners were not original in their structure or subject-matter, which were very much of the period. Their distinguishing features were the wit and brilliance which Wilde invested in the dialogue, characterised primarily by sparkling epigrams ("I can resist everything except temptation") and by clever inversion of clichés ("In married life three is company, two is none"), many of which have passed into the language.

Beneath the glittering wit, Wilde deals in the first three plays with questions of private and public morality, sometimes in a melodramatic and sentimental manner. In *Lady Windermere's Fan*, described by Wilde as "one of those drawing-room plays with pink lampshades", he explores questions of fidelity, reputation, and the nature of good and evil. In *A Woman of No Importance* the focus is on family secrets, in this case an illegitimate son, and the gap between what people say and what they mean. *An Ideal Husband*, the best of the three, tells the story of a politician whose wealth and reputation is based on a betrayal.

The director Tyrone Guthrie observed of *The Importance of Being Earnest*: "Though it's full of nonsense, it is also full of profound and utterly charming sense." In this delightful masterpiece Wilde casts aside all serious discussion of morality as well as the sentiment of the earlier plays. The result is a blissful concoction of wit and elegance, overflowing with memorable characters and observations. It is interesting, though hardly essential, to know that the play's dialogue reflects in code aspects of Wilde's own subterranean life. "Earnest" was apparently Victorian slang for "gay"; "Cicely" was a well-known name for rent boys; and "Bunbury", the fictitious relative, stood for some kind of double-life.

On the day Wilde was arrested, both *The Importance of Being Earnest* and *An Ideal Husband* were playing to packed houses in the West End. His tragic trial and imprisonment shattered his reputation, turning the public and most of his friends against him. On his death a journalist observed: "Nothing he ever wrote has the strength to endure." Yet his works – most notably the plays, but also the novels, children's stories and poems – continue to delight and stimulate, and will surely still do so a hundred years from now.

8

Theatre Companies

The National – Prospect – Adventures in Motion Pictures

Moving House

In 1976 the National moved from the Old Vic to its permanent home on the South Bank. Twenty-five years later I interviewed Diana Rigg and Denis Quilley to hear their views on the two theatres, and listened to Bill Bryden reminiscing about his years at the head of his "creative family" in the Cottesloe theatre.

Diana Rigg

I WAS IN ONE OF the last National companies at the Old Vic, along with Alec McCowen, Denis Quilley, Joan Plowright and Frank Finlay. Olivier, whom I loved and admired, was still around then, and quite robust. I remember him coming to all our run-throughs, and participating a lot.

The Vic was a glorious theatre to play in: it just gave you a present as soon as you stepped on to the stage. I loved its accessibility, its traditional shape. The highlight there for me was *Le Misanthrope*, because it was such a surprising hit. It was the first time a Molière play became a popular success, thanks to Tony Harrison's superb modern adaptation, and John Dexter's very fine production.

We had a few difficult moments. During the first preview of *Jumpers* the revolve got stuck. The delay seemed to go on for ever, and we were all feeling pretty gloomy. But Tom Stoppard had written a superb play, and when we got it together it was absolutely wonderful.

We were very close as a company, we felt part of one project. After the move from the Vic I did nothing at the National for twenty years. I don't remember feeling miffed or anything. But I was very much part of the old guard, I was bred and nurtured in the company process. Suddenly it seemed to disappear, to my great regret. So I wasn't sorry not to be part of the new set-up, though I knew it was a historic moment. Ironically it was also the moment that Peter Hall, who had resurrected the company ethos of the RSC, decided not to follow it any more.

When I came back in 1995, it was to do Brecht's *Mother Courage*. I thought the Olivier stage was awful, it was much too big and trundly for a play which had hundreds of small scenes. Subsequently the play was done elsewhere in a smaller theatre, where it was a huge success. It showed that you have to be really careful what you put into the Olivier.

I'm pleased to be back at the National for *Humble Boy*, especially as we're playing it in the Cottesloe; it's like being back in the Almeida. It's just a pity about the dressing-rooms: they're like battery-hen hatches, completely without character, very noisy, with little space or decent light. As actors we don't expect to be pampered, but we have to be in top form to go out and do it. The conditions are absolutely ludicrous for a theatre built from scratch. It makes me cross every time I enter the building.

Denis Quilley

At the Old Vic, Larry Olivier used to choose the play to fit round the company. Sometimes you had to bring in new people because of numbers, and sometimes the plays had only three or four characters. But basically it was an old-fashioned rep company, all of whom knew each other very well.

In a place the size of the South Bank you can't have the same kind of communal feeling. The circumstances are so different, it's not the same family situation. You can't do what Larry did, which was to train up people like Tony Hopkins and Ronnie Pickup from spear-carriers to stars.

When we finally opened the new building with *Hamlet* and *Tamburlaine the Great* there was a huge sense of relief. But the move, with all the long delays, was hair-raising. We must have rehearsed *Tamburlaine* for about four months; once we put it on outside just to keep ourselves amused. We even staged *Troilus and Cressida* at the Young Vic during rehearsals, to give us something to do while we waited.

Then one day we were all assembled on the Olivier stage, and Peter Hall announced that he finally had a firm opening date. We all cheered and clapped. A couple of hours later an underling came in and whispered in his ear. I'd never seen Peter lose his cool before: he picked up his script, threw it on the floor and jumped on it, cursing and swearing. He didn't need to tell us that it was yet another delay.

Albert Finney was playing both Hamlet and Tamburlaine. He was marvellous. One or two other actors I can think of might well have walked out in such circumstances, but he didn't. He never lost his temper, which was remarkable, because it was a long ordeal, terribly dispiriting and energy-sapping.

We played both productions in the Olivier. As soon as I stepped on to the stage I felt quite at home, and a tremendous sense of awe and excitement, which I still have. I don't get that in the Lyttelton, because I don't feel the same contact with the audience; it's as though we are in two separate compartments. It never gives me the sense of community that the Olivier does. There we are all sharing the same space, which I find very stimulating. I think it's the most wonderful theatre.

Bill Bryden

The meeting between the Cottesloe and myself was one of those marvellous happenstances. Peter Hall decided to have associate directors for all three theatres at the National, and offered me the Cottesloe. "Give it a personality," he said. That was fine: it seemed to me the theatre with the most potential, with the most unadorned, least rigid space.

It was not exactly a permanent company I had there, but more of a floating association of artists. People I had worked with at the Royal Court, such as Jack Shepherd and Brian Glover; musicians like John Tams, Ashley Hutchings and Martin Carthy; designers like William Dudley and Hayden Griffin. We were a creative family, with strong

Celtic and northern elements, a group of people who were together in their work and in their life, who cared very much about the National idea, but particularly about the Cottesloe.

We were very fortunate, because a lot of our work was very successful. Productions such as *The Mysteries, Lark Rise* and *Candleford* made our reputation. Of course it was easier to fill the Cottelsoe than the Lyttelton or the Olivier. But people who came knew there was a kind of guarantee – of personality, quality, energy, commitment.

Although it wasn't the same team for every production, there was a recognisable style of acting, and some of the players spent many months there. But sometimes we did "proper" plays as well. The company would be together, and then they would perhaps go off and do some television, and I would do a Mamet play such as *American Buffalo*.

There was definitely a following, a lot of people came regularly: the theatre was small enough for you to recognise them. And people who had been engaged when they came to the original productions of *The Mysteries* or *Lark Rise* brought their children along when we revived the plays.

If the Cottesloe had been in Stoke-on-Trent all this would have been perfectly normal. But it happened to be stuck on to the National Theatre in London, with access to the best actors, and that's what made it remarkable.

A Glittering Company

In the autumn of 2006 I wrote a short piece for an Old Vic programme on the tenure there of the Prospect Theatre Company. At the same time I had a lengthy interview with the company's artistic director Toby Robertson, who gave me his candid recollections of the ups and downs of the company's difficult years at the Old Vic. As a companion piece to the article, his memories are published here for the first time.

THE OLD VIC PLAYED HOST to many outstanding theatre companies during the second half of the twentieth century. The most celebrated of course was the National Theatre. Less well remembered or documented is the tenure of Prospect Theatre Company, which arrived under the artistic direction of Toby Robertson and, with a host of stars and actors on board, staged several acclaimed productions.

The company began life in 1961 at the Oxford Playhouse, where Prospect Productions was formed by Iain Mackintosh, Richard Cottrell and Elizabeth Sweeting. In 1964 Toby Robertson was made artistic director, and the company was based at the Arts in Cambridge. In 1967 it began a ten-year association with the Edinburgh Festival, and in 1969 it became the country's major touring company, changing its name to Prospect Theatre Company.

In the 1970s the company was mounting four productions a year: plenty of Shakespeare, but also other writers, including Chekhov, Turgenev, Otway and Wycherley. This led the Old Vic governors to invite Prospect to stage a season at the Vic commemorating the Queen's Jubilee in 1977, and soon after they announced "a marriage that is all but a merger" between Prospect and the Vic, with Toby Robertson being given artistic control of the theatre.

There were many memorable performances during this time, including Derek Jacobi's Hamlet, Ivanov and Sir Andrew Aguecheek; Eileen Atkins' Saint Joan and Viola;

Anthony Quayle's King Lear; and Ian Richardson as Gogol's Government Inspector. Other stars in this glittering company during the Vic years were Isla Blair, Robert Eddison, Julian Glover, Barbara Jefford, Alec McCowen, Geoffrey Palmer, Prunella Scales, Dorothy Tutin and Timothy West.

"I loved being at the Vic," Eileen Atkins remembers. "You always felt all the ghosts around, but I was never intimidated by the tradition, just inspired by it. And Toby was a wonderfully imaginative director, always very encouraging – though he'd say so if he thought you were bloody awful."

At one stage there were plans to take a leaf out of Lilian Baylis' book and bring in a ballet and opera company to share the Vic with Prospect. But they came to nothing, and the financial burden of running both a theatre and a touring company, together with disagreements over artistic policy, eventually led to Toby Robertson leaving in 1980. The company continued for a further year under Timothy West, until the Arts Council withdrew its grant, so ending Prospect's brief tenure at the Vic.

Toby Robertson

I came to Prospect in 1964 to direct *The Provok'd Wife*, with Eileen Atkins, Edward Hardwicke and Trevor Martin. After that production they asked me to join the company permanently. We then decided we couldn't have a base at Oxford, so we did a Zuleika Dobson in reverse, and went to Cambridge.

At the time we put on the first professional full-stage production of *The Provok'd Wife* at the newly reopened Georgian Theatre in Richmond in Yorkshire. This was fascinating to me, because I was brought up in Swaledale by my grandparents. I remember when I was about seven my grandfather took me in to the theatre, which was then a corn store. It had an amazing feeling.

We did five Prospect productions there, and it became an artistic base; it defined what we were, working in that small space. Iain Mackintosh then went on to design the Tricycle, the Wilde at Bracknell, and the Cottesloe – all based on the Georgian Theatre, except instead of a horseshoe shape, we suddenly got this rectangle. It had quite an important effect on theatre building.

Then we were invited to the Edinburgh Festival. We had a very strong association there for ten years with the Assembly Hall and the Lyceum. *The Provok'd Wife*, *The Cherry Orchard* and *The Beggar's Opera* all went to London, as did *Edward II* and *Richard II*. But in order to keep up the standard and attract the quality people, I felt there had to be a London base. And with people like Derek Jacobi and Eileen Atkins, we needed to have a showcase place.

We'd used the Roundhouse for quite a bit. But I could see the argument that there wasn't a vital need for another classical company in London. So we were working against the feeling from a lot of people that now we've got the National, we don't need the Vic any more. A lot of people were very against it: I discovered later that Peter Hall, then the National's director, hated the whole idea of us being at the Old Vic, because he didn't want to have another classical company just a mile down the road from the National.

He did *Hamlet* there with Albert Finney, while we did it with Derek. We had just three or four weeks for rehearsal, while the National had seven or eight. But there were about two hundred people outside the stage door at the Vic, and he didn't like that very much. There was always a good audience, but it was difficult for us working against another classical company.

So the whole thing became a most enormous political shemozzle, and as one of my chairmen said, I dug the hole, and they all jumped in! There was a big fuss, people like Marius Goring writing and saying that when the Vic Company under Michael Elliott stopped and the National came in, he swore that the Arts Council had said they would honour the Vic Company for the future, and put a classical company back into the Vic. But the council said they had no recollection of any such commitment.

If one was going to be in the Vic and yet be committed to touring, it was impossible to do both at the same time all year. We then had the idea of having an opera company and a ballet company and Prospect using it a third of a year each. That seemed sensible, but then sense doesn't always prevail: it's very much what the fashion is. The moment we did that the Arts Council pulled the money out of the English Opera Group with Colin Graham. Then there was the Ballet Rambert, but the council told them they shouldn't get involved. There was an awful lot of politicking going on: one was up against enormous problems, with not a penny of public money.

It became too much for everybody. I certainly found it a terrific strain. For example, I wanted to have an associate director – maybe Jonathan Miller or Patrick Garland – and they would only give me £12,000 a year. I wasn't going to get anybody of any real quality for that. There was the hope that Anthony Quayle might get more involved, but he was hankering after his own company, and set up Compass.

In 1969-70 we were asked to make ourselves a major Number One touring company, and so we split that into

Prospect and the Actors' Company, which Richard Cottrell went off to start. That's where the pot of money was, in the touring. There was a great demand around the country for seeing the classics. I'm always amazed how many people in Newcastle, Cardiff or Leeds I've met who say they first started going to the theatre with Prospect.

The early days were a big adventure, because we really were working on a shoestring, which was frightfully good for all of us. There wasn't much touring then, and we seemed to be fulfilling a real need in a lot of these places. As a touring company I suppose our motto was "Better to travel hopefully than to arrive" – but when we did arrive we didn't stay there very long, and that's the sadness.

At one point I think Frank Dunlop had an idea that the Young Vic might get involved. Michael Benthall was very helpful to me, trying to sort things out. But it was impossible. We had a very strong contact with the British Council, who also took us on. The whole trouble was basically financial. It was also mad. At one point there was simultaneously a company in Poole, Peking, Bradford and Berlin.

The Vic tied up well with the great provincial theatres, they all had a great compatibility with it. So that all made sense. The basic idea was to try and find some way of giving it a new lease of life. Michael Bogdanov brought three Shakespeare productions in under our aegis. The problem was trying to be responsible for the Vic for fifty-two weeks of the year while also touring. A touring company wasn't the solution, because we couldn't really afford to run London as well. We could pay for the productions through the touring budget, but running the Vic and the staff needed and everything else was just too much.

The Vic is the most wonderful theatre to play in

acoustically, and you also have that sense of a strong rapport with an audience. We tried to use an awful lot of the past: for example, if we did *Hamlet*, we talked about other *Hamlet*s, to make it part of a continuity. We tried to get Gielgud and Olivier and such people to do anything they could to help, and on the whole they were very good, and very helpful. But it was an exhausting time, going out to dinner after rehearsals and getting up and talking to people who might support the Vic.

I think we were the only other English company playing at the Aldwych after the RSC. We did *King Lear* with Timothy West and *Love's Labour's Lost* in the early or mid 1970s. Some of the work was very fine. *The Government Inspector* was great fun, and Ian Richardson was wonderful: people think of him as a cold actor, but he was one of the best farceurs I have seen. When the company was in Newcastle, Barbara Jefford's wig fell off, and Ian did the most brilliant monologue for three or four minutes, while she went off stage and had it put on again.

Of my own productions, one I remember particularly was *Ivanov* with Derek, which I thought was excellent. There was also an adaptation of Christopher Logue's *War Music*, which was really interesting. But it was ahead of its time: people weren't interested in a theatre company almost being a dance company.

Derek played Sir Andrew in *Twelfth Night*, and was wonderful. The great thing about Derek was that he was the most terrific character actor; he always got under the skin of his characters. He was a very good Hamlet. He's very intelligent, and he brought a lot of passion to the part. Derek is incredibly generous in rehearsal, and usually turns up knowing his part, so that he's a bit ahead of everybody; but he also leads people through.

Eileen Atkins is more private, but she does set a standard. Her quality has always been her extraordinary repose on stage. She's the most economical actress I've ever come across. She has a complete clarity of where she wants to go. Lesser actors need to be encouraged and brought through, and that comes as much from a company as it does from a director. There was quite an ensemble feel to it.

A lot of people had a good bite at good things early on in their careers. Ian McKellen made his first big mark with the *Edward II / Richard II* double-bill. Timothy West totally came up through Prospect, notably with his Bolingbroke and Mortimer. We also had people like Robert Eddison and Barbara Jefford: I never understood why she hasn't received a damehood, but then perhaps she doesn't want it?

It was quite a sudden rise for Prospect. After *Edward II* and *Richard II* – which went from Edinburgh to the Mermaid and the Piccadilly – we weren't quite sure whether to carry on. Do we go on with the slog, or do we go and do something else? There was a feeling that it would be rather sad to lose what we had achieved, so we carried on.

We learnt a certain simplicity, which meant we could go to, say, Peking with just a bundle of drapes, and that was the set. It really was a bare stage most of the time. We also got much more involved musically; we spent quite a bit of money on having a permanent set of musicians at the Vic. It was very exciting, and it allowed one to do an awful lot of things that one wouldn't be able to do otherwise.

We did *The Padlock* and *Miss in Her Teens* as a double-bill for the Garrick centenary; no one else was doing anything. They were one-act operettas, and that wasn't considered quite the thing. We were told: "If you're running a classical theatre company, would you please run a classical theatre company, and not go off and do things like *War Music*." I certainly wasn't keeping to a commercially classical programme; it was a bit hither and thither, and not very conventional.

Looking back, it was too much of a one-man band, which was not what I wanted it to be. I left in 1980 because the board wanted me to go: there was a palace revolution while I was away in Peking. I think they thought I was intolerable because I wouldn't say no to anybody. It was very much a bums-on-seats time, Thatcher and all that, and they weren't so interested in the artistic side.

They then suggested Timothy West take over. I said, He's never run a company in his life, he's not a director or anything, I don't think this is sensible. But he did take over, and within a year Prospect stopped – though it could be argued that it was me who had dug the hole!

A New Level of Realism

In 2000 Matthew Bourne and his innovative company Adventures in Motion Pictures staged the dance/thriller The Car Man, *which then toured nationally and internationally for three years. On the occasion of its revival for yet another tour, he explained to me why he was keen to get away from the fantasy of his earlier shows, and stage a piece more raw and real.*

AFTER HIS RADICAL MAKEOVER OF classics of the ballet canon – *Nutcracker, Swan Lake, Cinderella* – Matthew Bourne's *The Car Man*, an imaginative reworking and updating of Bizet's much-loved opera *Carmen*, electrified critics and audiences alike. In the *Evening Standard* awards for 2000, his exhilarating dance/thriller was judged the Musical Event of the Year.

Now he's reviving this explosive hit show, which shifts the action from a cigarette factory in nineteenth-century Spain to the 1960s, and a greasy garage and diner in a small Mid-West American town, where lust, revenge and murder are the abiding passions. What then has led him to choose this powerful story for his acclaimed New Adventures company?

"I wanted to do something where the dancers were portraying characters closer to themselves," he explains. "They had spent a long time playing princesses and princes, so I felt it would be nice for them to play young, sexy people for a change, characters they could identify with more." He was always keen to get away from fantasy. "*Swan Lake* and *Cinderella* relied on that quite heavily – big sections of them were in the mind. I was looking for a story that was raw and real. *Carmen* was screaming out to be done."

He created the story himself, initially setting it in a meat factory, but deciding this would be too raw. It was film that finally provided the solution. A fan of *film noir* and the Italian neo-realists, at the time he was watching early Visconti classics. "It's such a rich area of film, with a very operatic way of acting and storytelling," he suggests. "I like the dirty, earthy characters. So the show begins with a set-up like *The Postman Only Rings Twice*, before going its own way."

He believes his company made a great leap forward during the three years *The Car Man* toured nationally and internationally. "The dancers grew substantially; I think they reached a new level of realism in their work." Some of this he puts down to his insistence that members of the chorus write their characters' life-histories, deciding who they are, why they have come to the town, how they relate to the other characters, and much else.

A youthful 47, and celebrating twenty years at the head of his independent dance company, now based at Sadler's Wells, he believes *The Car Man* brought in a new audience. "It won over lots of people to dance: people gave it a try, and now they've become more regular fixtures. Because the dancers looked like real people rather than phoney, silky fairies, the audience fell in love with them. It had a very big impact."

9

Theatre Projects

NT2000 Platforms – Ken Campbell's Comedy
Skills Workshop – Transformation – Royal Court
Young Writers' Festival – Edinburgh Fringe –
Playwriting Competition – The National's Studio

NT2000: A Century of Plays

At the start of the new millennium the National launched an
ambitious series of Platforms, featuring the most significant
plays of the last century. I attended the first three evenings,
devoted to works by Barrie, Barker and Synge.

VARIETY AND RICHNESS ARE THE keynotes of NT2000, and
both were in evidence in the initial Platforms staged at the
National at the start of the year. Could you have three more
contrasting plays than J. M. Barrie's *Peter Pan*, Harley

Granville Barker's *The Voysey Inheritance*, and J. M. Synge's *The Playboy of the Western World*?

The series began with a real coup: the first public performance of the final scene from the first draft of *Peter Pan*, read by the current National cast. Set in Kensington Gardens, full of the Barrie charm, it has Hook disguised as a schoolmaster (the crocodile still gets him!), and Wendy and Peter playing truant from school. Andrew Birkin, the author of the riveting book *J. M. Barrie and the Lost Boys*, touched on several aspects of the play's history – how Hook didn't feature in the first draft, how Barrie continually rewrote scenes, why he donated the royalties from the play to the Great Ormond Street Children's Hospital, and why Nina Boucicault burst into tears on the first night. It was fascinating stuff.

The Voysey Inheritance prompted a more serious, scholarly session, which was as much about the man as about the play. Two short extracts underlined Barker's pre-occupation with fundamental moral and social questions, while the discussion picked up on his all-round talent as director, Shakespeare scholar, manager and campaigner, as well as playwright.

Margery Morgan, a Barker expert, suggested provocatively that without him the National would not have come into being. "No one had such a burning passion about it," she argued. So why, asked a member of the audience, was no theatre in the building named after him?

Next up was Synge's poetic masterpiece, wonderfully brought to life by Stephen Rea and Fiona Shaw, who read two key scenes between Christy Mahon and Pegeen Mike, and quickly drew us into Synge's intoxicating language.

Bill Bryden, who directed the National's 1975 production, read from Synge's stirring introduction to the play.

Neither he nor Stephen Rea, who starred in it, expressed a wish to recreate the production. But with such a flowering of Irish playwrights taking place, it's surely time for a revival of what Stephen Rea called "the finest Irish play we have"?

Three down, only ninety-seven to go. What better way could there be to have a crash course in twentieth-century theatre history than these informative, entertaining Platforms?

Surreal Jokes and Practical Insights

Ken Campbell has been described as 'the maverick's maverick'. I watched the subversive and eccentric performer in action in the summer of 1995, as he tried to instil comedy skills into a bunch of London teenagers.

MOST DRAMA TEACHERS TEND TO adopt a gentle approach when trying to improve a student's performance. This is not Ken Campbell's way. "I don't call it directing, I call it abuse," he says. "I like to do it loudly, to make an event of it."

We're in the basement at the Royal Academy of Dramatic Art, in the small George Bernard Shaw theatre. A couple of dozen students from London schools are reaching the end of a fortnight's summer school organised by the National Theatre, during which they have been picking up comedy skills from the maverick writer and entertainer, and working on some of his bizarre, loony sketches. Now it's time for notes.

"Don't for God's sake present us with that kind of crap," Ken Campbell says to one boy, glaring from under his bushy eyebrows. "You seem not to have listened to anything I've told you in the last few days. You've decided to experiment by doing the exact opposite of what I've said, and you've given us a real plughole performance."

This and other equally candid comments seem to be taken on board quite happily by this group of older teenagers. They admit they've not met anyone like Ken Campbell in their school: they respect his brutal honesty, they relish his randiness, and they enjoy his lack of respect for authority. "He's anti-establishment, so you can relate to him," one girl says. Another adds: "He's got so much to pass on, but he's really unpredictable, so you have to be alert all the time." A boy observes: "He may humiliate you, but when he praises you, you know it must be significant."

Looking for all the world like a belligerent pixie, beneath the eccentricity Ken Campbell is actually a hard-nosed, energetic professional, with a real concern for matters of stagecraft. In weekly rep, where he served his time for several years, he recalls learning it automatically: today, he reckons, most actors and directors don't know the first thing about it.

"I'm only interested in things that are funny," he says. "But comedy isn't difficult for those who want to be funny. You just have to find the natural comedy in people. I've been trying to get the kids to be aware of the little moments – a beat, a tone, a move – which are so important, but where things can go so easily wrong."

During the fortnight the students have been learning some of the basics, with specific reference to comedy acting: how to come in through a door, how to make a double take, how to avoid "hiding" on stage, how to produce tears at a moment's notice. But there have also been more Campbell-esque exercises, such as creating characters out of the two halves of your face, with the aid of a mirror; telling tall stories or delivering monologues; or indulging in wordplay. He's also got the students to analyse the different kinds of laughter, from the titter to the guffaw, that come from an audience, and has suggested ways of using what they find – as a professional comic such as Ken Dodd does.

The sketches, many from *The Ken Campbell Roadshow*, offer the students plenty of scope for honing their comic skills. A girl turns into a hen and lays an egg; a man has a dialogue with his paunch; a nun receives a pornographic letter; a bag lady relieves a would-be suicide of his trousers; a man disappears up his backside.

Although he's not worked with young people before, Ken Campbell clearly has a way with them. It's a technique that is totally unpatronising, that allows for no inhibitions in the performers ("Either you do this bit or you go home, David"), that mixes surreal jokes with practical insights, and keeps everyone on their toes. The students loved it.

Brave New Season

During the summer of 2002, for the National's Transformation season, two new theatre spaces were created within the building. With the transformed Lyttelton and new Loft theatre about to open, I reported on the thinking behind this bold experiment, and talked to directors Mick Gordon and Kathryn Hunter about their contrasting shows.

AFTER MONTHS OF PLANNING, NEGOTIATION and rehearsing, the Transformation season has begun. The first show in the transformed Lyttelton is an original theatrical take on Jeannette Winterson's novel *The PowerBook*, set in London, Paris, Capri and Cyberspace. Meanwhile, up in the new Lyttelton Loft, Rory Williams' *Sing Yer Heart Out for the Lads* is the first of eight new plays to be staged in the intimate space carved out of the former Lyttelton exhibition area.

An ambitious venture involving thirteen world premieres, Transformation is all about encouraging younger writers and directors to work at the National. But it also represents an attempt to attract a new audience to the South Bank, while offering a wider range of work to the existing audience. While the Loft concentrates on new writing, the focus in the transformed Lyttelton is on "made theatre", with productions created from a variety of sources.

"We wanted to allow significant theatre artists to experiment more freely in the larger space, to allow the National to engage in their work in progress," says Mick Gordon, the season's associate director. Among the artists who have been drawn into the project are Deborah Warner and Fiona Shaw (directing and acting in Jeannette Winterson's *The PowerBook*), Kathryn Hunter in collaboration with Mamaloucos Circus, Matthew Bourne, and Trestle Theatre Company.

Kathryn Hunter is currently working with Peter Brook at the Bouffes du Nord in Paris. "I think it's a very brave and imaginative step for the National to take," she says. "I know viscerally that the Lyttelton is very difficult to play in, because it's such a divided space. The transformed version, with the stalls joined to the circle, is much more unified. It's not like a studio, but it feels very embraceable, while retaining the élan of a big space."

Her own contribution to the season is a circus-theatre adaptation of Aristophanes' *The Birds*, for which she will direct a mixed company of actors and circus performers. The script, by Sean O'Brien, is a racy, colloquial and very funny modern-verse version of the classic Greek comedy. "I love the play, but the existing versions had a terrible antiqueness," she observes. "It was hard to cross the bridge from the ancient world of Greek tragedy and comedy to our modern world. Sean triumphed here, winging his way effortlessly between the two worlds."

She's been involved in versions of the project for two years, and is passionate on the subject of circus. "It's regarded as a great art-form in France and other European countries, but in England there's not the same appreciation. Yet I think it's poetry in motion, and provides as much soul-food as the more traditional, text-based theatre."

She started developing the idea of the project with Mamaloucos, a company which develops original circus-theatre productions. The idea was initially workshopped with the company, and it is hoped that after the run at the National the production will tour to several venues around the UK in a Mamaloucos tent.

The need to find circus performers with acting skills has led to a big search in England and France, and lots of auditions. There have been workshops, with and without circus equipment; last year a group spent time at the National's Studio exploring some of the key situations in the play. The resulting fifteen-strong company is a young one. "Their youthful outlook will permeate the piece," Kathryn Hunter suggests.

Challenging in a different way will be the season's second production, an adaptation of *A Prayer for Owen Meany*. John Irving's extraordinary epic American novel, spanning three generations and including the Vietnam era, tells the story of an undersized boy with a wrecked voice who believes he is God's instrument. The process of transforming this complex, tragi-comic work into a piece of theatre is being undertaken by writer Simon Bent in conjunction with Mick Gordon, who is also directing the production.

As the latter explained: "I originally asked for the rights four years ago to do it at the Gate Theatre in Notting Hill. But on reflection I felt the Gate was too small to realise some of the images that were crucial to the story, such as the baseball game or the Nativity Play."

The decision to focus on the relationship between faith and religion inevitably means certain scenes and issues have had to be dropped, although much of the political material remains. "The novel is structurally meandering, which I don't think is interesting in the theatre," he suggests. "Our job has been to sharpen it, and to choose moments in which many themes are examined through character and narrative action."

Casting the part of Owen Meany involved a difficult choice. Should they opt for an American child with a squeaky voice, find an actor with a physical quirk or disability, or just go for the best actor available, and find ways of making him convincing as a youngster? "The third option seemed to be the most appropriate and practical – and also the most fun for the director," Mick Gordon admits.

The innovative Lyttelton season contains two further productions. Trestle will perform *The Adventures of the Stoneheads*, Toby Wilsher's mask epic, which he will direct. To end the season Matthew Bourne, who won an Olivier award for his sizzling choreography of *My Fair Lady* at the National, is radically developing his narrative dance work *Play Without Words*, his first production since he established his company New Adventures.

Strategies for Survival

The Royal Court Young Writers' Festival has long been a seedbed for budding playwrights. In 1992 I spoke to Jonathan Harvey and four other playwrights, to discover how their careers had gone since they had taken part in the festival.

"MY FRIENDS THINK GETTING A job like teaching is spoiling my creativity. They're probably right." During the day Jonathan Harvey is a probationary teacher at a London comprehensive. Only in the evenings and at weekends can he revert to his first career, that of playwriting.

Finance is just one of the problems facing young playwrights. Isolation is another. Jonathan and the four others I talked to – Marie Oshodi, Sean Duggan, Hannah Vincent and Jyoti Patel – all participated in the Royal Court Young Writers' Festival. With such a start how have they fared since?

All five have in fact been relatively successful and have continued as writers, even if some of them have had to take other work. While Jonathan teaches English at Abbey Wood School in Greenwich, Marie is writing her fourth play while doing a drama degree at Middlesex Polytechnic, and Hannah works in a Brighton bookshop three days a week. The other two manage to write full-time.

Inevitably, most of them have turned their hand to film, video or television, to make up for the modest sums to be gained from theatre work. Sean Duggan's career, for example, shows the kind of mixture a young writer needs in order to survive.

In 1986, at the age of 15, he had his first play *William* accepted for the festival. As a member of the Everyman Youth Theatre in Liverpool, he only saw the leaflet about the festival just before the closing date for entries, and with the boldness of youth dashed the play off in a couple of days. The story of a Liverpool lad wanting to escape his surroundings, it has been produced in at least one venue every year since.

He then wrote *A Brisk Affair* for Liverpool Playhouse, *You Lucky Swine* for the BBC's Debut on Two series, and a short play for Channel 4, *High Rise, Low Life*. He is currently working on a full-length play for Sandie Shaw loosely based on her life ("She'd read *William*, we had tea, and ended up making these mad plans"), and a one-hour film for Channel 4 about the fantasies of a girl living in New Brighton. He's also been approached to write for *Brookside*.

"It's always been natural for me to write plays – my mum claims I've been doing it since I was seven," he says. "But I don't set out to write a particular kind of piece. I just like to take some real characters in real situations and see what happens." He confesses to feeling quite isolated working from home.

This is one problem that Jyoti Patel does not have. Since her play *Awhha* (*Voices*) was performed at the festival in 1986, most of her writing has been in collaboration with Jezz Simons, a teacher at Soar Valley Community College in Leicester, where she lives. Their method is to work out a play's structure together, share out the individual scenes, and then act as critics for each other. "I don't know how writers manage working on their own," she says. "It's much more stimulating having someone else's ideas as well. You row a lot, but it works."

Most of their work is about and for the Asian community, and uses English and Gujarati, which they both speak. They've had plays on at the Leicester Haymarket Studio, the RSC, Battersea Arts Centre, Soho Poly and elsewhere, and are now writing one for the Bush. They've also recently written episodes of *EastEnders*.

Jyoti, now 20, has kept in touch with younger people by doing workshops of her plays in schools. For Marie Oshodi, contact has been through a different route. Last year she worked with Paddington Arts, writing scenes for a full-length video for a mixed cast of professionals and young people aged seven and upwards, helping them to move on from improvisation to the script stage.

Marie was 19 when her first, autobiographical play, *The S Bend*, about a Nigerian girl in London and her search for a cultural identity, had a rehearsed reading at the festival in 1984. "Before that I had the usual stereotype view of the theatre as an elitist, middle-class place," she admits. "But the festival gave me a lot of insight into what was possible."

Partially sighted at the time, she is now able to see very little, and works with a four-track cassette recorder. Her disability has not prevented her from writing several stage plays, a television piece, and three plays for schools. She's now working on one about blindness for the Graeae Theatre Company, and has just completed twenty interviews with David Blunkett and other less-well-known blind people.

Her plays deal with social issues facing young people, including disability and unemployment. Much the same goes for Jonathan Harvey, who comes from Liverpool. His second play, *Mohair*, was in the 1988 festival. "It was a time when *Letter to Brezhnev* and *Boys from the Blackstuff* showed that people from Liverpool could write about ordinary things," he recalls.

His output since then includes several plays, some work for television and the script of a safe-sex video for a local health authority, and he is currently working on a novel. "I write on things I feel strongly about, like the working-class struggle," he says. "Also on being poor – I know a lot about that, being a teacher."

Hannah Vincent's play *The Burrow* was performed at the festival in 1988, when she was 21. Since then she's written a play for the Orange Tree Youth Theatre in Richmond and, among other work, a devised piece for the Royal Court Young People's Theatre on AIDS and HIV, *Throwing Stones*, which was taken into schools.

"We did it the Joint Stock way, with everyone researching and then me having to go away and write it in four weeks – a horrific responsibility," she says. In fact she liked working with the team. "It's difficult working alone. You need the comfort of others around you, and contact with normal people."

Recently she, Sean and Jonathan and other festival graduates went to the Interplay Festival in Australia, held for the most promising young playwrights from around the world. Here, Jonathan remembers, was the ideal antidote to isolation: "It was really good to be with other writers and to have people living and breathing your play. It was like going to a party."

Women and Writers First

While editing Arts Express magazine I spent a week in 1984 at the Edinburgh Festival Fringe, sampling many of the smaller solo shows on offer.

IT WAS A VERY INDIVIDUALISTIC and literary Fringe this year. While Virginia Woolf held forth in the genteel surroundings of the Caledonian Club, George Orwell was down and out twice a day at the Lyceum Studio. Elsewhere,

Jean-Jacques Rousseau was melancholic at the Traverse, Dashiell Hammett hard-boiled at the Herriot-Watt, and Dylan Thomas extremely bawdy in the Canongate.

If you missed these writers, you could bump into George Sand, Ivan Turgenev, Gertrude Stein or Mrs Thrale, and find them telling you their life story. Shakespeare, ever the enigma, chose not to appear in person, though plenty of his plays were on offer in Edinburgh. Instead he sent his Irish cousin, one O'Shakespeare. Meanwhile an eminent real-life Irishman contrived to be present in two theatres at the same time. To find one evening of Oscar may be regarded as good fortune (except it wasn't), but to find two...

Theatre was almost as well represented as literature. While Sarah Bernhardt (disguised as French screen star Delphine Seyrig) opted for the official festival, the Fringe was visited by Lillian Hellman, Marie Lloyd and Ellen Terry (two manifestations each) and Lilian Baylis. And from the world beyond the stage came Amelia Earhart (Aviation), Marie Stopes (Birth Control and Sexual Fulfilment) and James Miranda Barry (Medicine).

Most of those playing celebrated men and women chose to perform solo, either through lack of money or adequate theatre space, or both. This seems to be a growing phenomenon, much suited to the lean and hungry eighties. But it's a format that puts immense pressure on the performer, especially in the smaller spaces found within the Fringe. With the audience literally within spitting distance, they can ill afford any lapse in concentration, error of timing, or extraneous "business".

Of the ten shows I caught during the third week of the festival, the more literary productions were the least satisfying. Virginia Woolf's introspections, combined with extracts from her novels, did not make for a theatrical experience, despite Gabrielle Hamilton's efforts to provide one. Neither did it help if the production took the form of a lecture or series of readings, as with Denis Rafter's *The Remarkable Oscar Wilde* (Pleasance), which was chiefly remarkable for achieving the impossible feat of making Wilde charmless and unfunny.

The three shows that worked best had no direct connection with literature and, as it happened, were all performed by women. Polly March, in *Beauty and the Bounders* (Netherbow Arts Centre), offered an illuminating portrait of Lilian Baylis, conveying poignantly the sad personal life of the pioneering woman who brought opera and theatre to the people at the Old Vic. Similarly Pauline Devaney, who wrote and performed *To Marie with Love* (Pleasance), memorably caught the egotism and insensitivity of Marie Stopes, and her success in campaigning for women's right to sexual happiness and contraception. (The best time to insert a pessary, she told an audience of working-class mothers, was "just before dressing for dinner".)

The lives of formidable women often seem suitable for theatrical treatment, perhaps none more so than that of James Miranda Barry. Frederic Mohr's *Barry* (Traverse) made excellent use of this extraordinary story – a woman forced to live as a man for some sixty years in order to follow a career in medicine. Gerda Stevenson, playing Barry first as a woman and then as a man, gave a performance of rare beauty and subtlety, helped by a fine script that raised a two-hour monologue to drama of the highest quality.

Two other one-woman shows stood out, though in very different ways. Franca Rame's four monologues *It's All Bed, Board and Church* (Assembly Rooms) abounded in sharp comments on the sexual slavery of modern woman, and were played with a wonderful mixture of raw passion and humour. She and her husband Dario Fo have played to all kinds of audiences in Italy: what a shame that over here they should only reach the usual middle-class theatregoers.

Another show that certainly deserves a wider audience was *Behind the Oilscape* (Traverse). Using a rich selection of Scots and Gaelic songs, exquisitely sung and skilfully presented, Anne Lorne Gillies offered a moving but unsentimental people's history, and a refreshing antidote to the conventional tartan and heather image being peddled in other parts of Edinburgh during the festival.

The Play's the Thing

A 2006 playwriting competition to find a new West End talent attracted an impressive number of scripts from a cross-section of previously unproduced British writers. Producer Sonia Friedman and playwright Stephen Jeffreys explained to me the nature of the work submitted, and the process the shortlisted writers went through.

SINCE THE OPENING OF THE National Theatre no play by a first-time playwright has come straight into London's West End and achieved success. Kate Betts' *On the Third Day* will, Sonia Friedman hopes, break that regrettable mould.

"It's a play about faith in the twenty-first century, about how people living in a busy world get through and survive in a crisis," she says. "There's a lot going on in it, both theatrically and visually: it has a large beating heart at its centre which will appeal to a wide audience."

A teacher from Chichester in her late forties, Kate Betts has emerged as the winner of the playwriting competition

"The Play's the Thing", the subject in June of a four-part Channel 4 series. It attracted an impressive two thousand scripts from previously unproduced British-based writers, who included teachers, shop workers, graduates, scientists, call-centre workers, unemployed actors, restaurateurs and many others.

"It was a complete cross-section of society in relation to race, background, class and education," Sonia Friedman emphasises. "This meant we got a very broad range of work, and many different styles and genres. Most of the plays in the top thirty were domestic one-set dramas, but there were a couple of attempts at big, knockabout farce, and three political plays."

The writers had first to submit a synopsis and sample scenes, which were read by a team of professional readers. A chosen thirty then met a panel of experts – literary agent Mel Kenyon, actor Neil Pearson and Sonia Friedman – who selected the final ten. These writers then worked intensively for four days, developing their material with the help of playwright Stephen Jeffreys. "It was a very interesting bunch of plays, and I think a couple of the writers have a long-term future," he says. "I tried to stress to them that a playwright has to be good at all the ingredients – structure, character, dialogue, the visual elements – and so they needed to look at what they were *not* good at in order to improve."

The writers then wrote a first draft, the panel reduced their number to three, and the winning play was chosen. Its director is Robert Delamere, and it stars Paul Hilton and Maxine Peake. "I hope this will open up the discussion about new writing in the West End," Sonia Friedman says. "We are being left behind by the subsidised sector, so we badly need to be nurturing new talent."

A Unique Laboratory

The National's Studio provides a valuable space for actors, writers and directors to develop their work. In the year 2000 I wrote about the range of opportunities on offer there, including a fruitful partnership between the Studio and the Gate theatre in Notting Hill.

TAKE A TOPICAL QUESTION: the crisis in verse-speaking and the handling of classical texts. Bring together under one roof four experts on the subject: John Barton, Peter Hall, Adrian Noble and Trevor Nunn. Mix in 150 theatre practitioners from all over the country. Allow to simmer for three weeks, meanwhile folding in twenty-one workshops run by leading actors.

The recent stimulating all-day forum on this subject, together with the extensive follow-up programme, was a typical Studio initiative. It's the kind of event that generally goes unnoticed by press or public, but is of incalculable value to the theatre people that the Studio was set up to serve.

Based since it was founded in 1984 in the Old Vic Annexe (which the National bought last year), the Studio is the National's vital research and development centre. It exists to encourage new writing; to offer space to directors, writers, actors and designers who want to do some exploratory or investigative work; and to run free tutorial classes for present and past members of the National's company. These three strands inevitably overlap and interconnect, resulting in a heady mixture of people, cutting-edge projects and activities.

Attachments for writers have been one of the Studio's success stories. Jonathan Harvey, Judith Johnson, Martin

McDonagh and Joe Penhall are among the many writers who have benefited from the scheme. "It's like a wonderful oasis, where you can work free of the usual deadlines," says Simon Block, who was given a room at the Studio, and wrote a complete play during his two-month attachment.

Sometimes an attachment may precede or follow a commission. The present aim is to have two writers at work at any one time, and so support around twelve a year. Sponsorship is now being sought for the scheme as a whole, or for individual attachments, which cost £2,000 each.

Young directors are also helped, either with an attachment, or through a chance to take part in the annual three-week young-directors' programme, which consists of workshops with leading practitioners. Debra Yhip from Liverpool, who has been assistant director at the Traverse in Edinburgh and with Theatre de Complicite, is halfway through an attachment.

"It's an ideal platform on which to build your work," she says. "It's like being in a laboratory: you can explore new ideas, watch experienced directors at work, and get to meet them, some of them being of international standing such as Peter Brook and Robert Lepage."

As the Studio's head Sue Higginson puts it succinctly: "The problem for young directors is to move on from doing *King Lear* in the pub with five people, to tackling a production on a main stage in Sheffield or Birmingham."

One small solution is the Direct Action project, which she has dreamed up in conjunction with David Lan, artistic director of the Young Vic. As a result two talented directors will get the chance to work for the first time in something larger than the studios and small theatres they are used to.

It's a beautifully simple collaboration. While the Studio funds the actors', directors' and designers' salaries during preparation and rehearsals, the Young Vic offers a good-size stage, and pays for the productions and running costs. "It's a fantastic opportunity for the directors, but it also enables us to do work we wouldn't otherwise be able to do," David Lan says.

The first two plays are interesting choices in themselves, neither having been seen in London for many years. First off is David Rudkin's *Afore Night Comes*, to be directed by Rufus Norris. Then comes *Andorra* by Max Frisch, staged at the National in 1964, and now directed by Gregory Thompson.

"The Studio is fantastic. It should be franchised all around the country." Director Indhu Rubasingham is a passionate enthusiast for the Studio. Recently she was part of a small group which took part in an extended workshop there with Peter Brook. For ten days they looked at texts from the founding fathers of modern theatre – Stanislavsky, Artaud, Craig, Meyerhold – shared ideas about them, and tested the theories by improvising scenes. The group included writers Lee Hall and Patrick Marber, director Mick Gordon, and actress Kathryn Hunter, as well as directors from abroad.

"The workshop was terribly valuable," Indhu Rubasingham says, "because it made you look at your work through other people's eyes. It was fascinating, for instance, to see what Stanislavsky meant to a Georgian director coming from a very different theatre tradition. It was also a rare chance for me to talk in depth with other directors I know, but have never seen in action."

Much of the Studio's work extends beyond the National's own repertoire. There's the annual residency at the Edinburgh Fringe, and an ambitious programme of new plays, co-produced with the Royal Court, for which Sue

Higginson and her colleagues read many scripts, and housed and funded the preparatory work.

Mick Gordon is brimming over with enthusiasm about his theatre's association with the National. Theatres don't come much smaller than the Gate in Notting Hill, a pub theatre with a fine reputation out of all proportion to its minute size. But its present six-month season of five new plays owes much to the unobtrusive and untrumpeted support of the Studio.

"It really makes us feel good that Big Brother is keeping an eye on the little people," says the Gate's artistic director. "It's a magic, very special link." The collaboration is part of the National's ongoing Springboards new-writing project. As with all such co-productions, the Studio is involved in the selection of plays, and supports the preparation and rehearsal period.

The earlier collaboration with the Royal Court led to a successful season of new British plays at the Ambassador's theatre in the West End. The Gate's season *Remembering the Future* differs slightly in that the plays, all British premieres, are by writers from four different continents. They were chosen from over a hundred scripts read by Mick Gordon, Sue Higginson and Jack Bradley, the National's literary manager.

The first three plays were Philip Kan Gotanda's Japanese story *Ballad of Yachiyo*, Matt Cameron's Australian memory play *Tear from a Glass Eye*, and the Italian writer Giuseppe Manfridi's sensational take on the Oedipus story, *Cuckoos*. The current production is *Pera Palas* by the Turkish writer Sinan H. Unel, and the season ends with the Argentinian poet Jorge Accame's play *Venecia*. The short-listed plays were given a reading at the Studio, and two workshops then helped to fix a final decision. "It was easy to agree because we all liked the same plays best," Mick Gordon recalls.

He's delighted to have netted Peter Hall as the director for the controversial *Cuckoos*. "I asked him if he would come and do it for us for £200, and he said okay. No one else will let him do it, it's too risky, too naughty. I thought if I directed it, it would just be seen as a young person being steamy. With Peter it will have more of an edge." Unusually, there are more women directors than men: Erica Whyman (*Tears from a Glass Eye*), Sasha Wares (*Pera Palas*) and Rebecca Gatwood, the Gate's new associate director (*Venetia*), are joined by James Kerr (*Ballard of Yachiyo*) and Peter Hall.

"What's fantastic is that for once we are able to pay actors something," Mick Gordon says. "As we have no money they usually just get travel cards, and lunches that we make for them during rehearsals. So we're really indebted to the Studio for covering the rehearsal money." But he believes it's not just the Gate that benefits from the association. "It means we can give a public face to work that goes on at the Studio that nobody knows about. We're also able to do plays that are too small to stage even in the Cottesloe."

He knows the Studio of old, having been on attachment there four years ago, the first director to have been awarded a bursary supported by the John S. Cohen Foundation. "I adore the place," he confesses. "I feel incredibly comfortable there. It's very stimulating and helpful, mixing with all the artists around the building. And it encourages you to be maverick."

The Studio's facilities include a large, medium and small space. But now that the National owns the annexe, thoughts are turning to a little gentle refurbishment and, more excitingly, to the possibility of creating a new, seventy-five-seat theatre within the building, open to the public at perhaps a nominal £2 a seat.

"It would be a place that would be commercially quite unviable, that could be used flexibly, that wouldn't need to be open all the time," Sue Higginson says. "A place where dangerous and extraordinary things could take place, where you could show work that had reached a certain level, and could benefit from being shown to a small paying audience before being exposed to the larger world outside." Sponsorship would certainly be needed to realise this dream. But a space has already been identified within the building that could be converted for use as a theatre.

In this hotbed of innovation, a key feature is unpredictability. "You never quite know when work done here will inform something for the future," says Sue Higginson. 'The general swilling around of artists produces surprising outcomes that you would never predict."

10

Ideas in Action

Women Directors – Theatre-in-the-Round –
Experimental Theatre – Music Theatre – Ensemble

Towards a Level Playing-Field

In the autumn of 2006 three of the plays being staged at the
National were being directed by women: Katie Mitchell,
Marianne Elliott and Melly Still. They talked to me about
the improved opportunities for women directors, the
difficulties that remain, and the hopeful signs for the future.

ACCORDING TO THE 1989 GULBENKIAN report *A Better*
Direction, twenty-nine per cent of directors in theatre in the
previous year were women. In the eighteen years since then
a growing number has entered the field, and several women
have become artistic directors. So is there now a genuine

equality of opportunity for women wanting to direct?

"There are still fewer women in the field than men, but in the ten years I've been directing it's changed a lot," Marianne Elliott says. "Although some theatres employ very few women directors, I don't think there's much prejudice out there now." Melly Still agrees: "I've not been aware of any prejudice, and I've had nothing but support from artistic directors," she says.

The opening on the three National stages this autumn of productions by women is clearly something of a landmark. "It's very exciting and delightful that there's this sudden rush of female directors coming up," Katie Mitchell says. Yet this welcome fact needs to be put in context: of the sixteen directors whose work has been or will be seen at the National during 2006, only four are women.

Children are inevitably a major factor in the equation. "Not many women with kids can direct, unless they don't need to worry about money, or have a partner who doesn't mind doing most of the childcare," says Marianne Elliott. "And even then it's unlikely, because a director's wage alone won't support a family."

Childcare can impose a financial strain. Katie Mitchell, who has a ten-month-old daughter, observes: "It's incredibly expensive, because what the government offers you is risible." Melly Still, with three children, puts it more starkly. "All my money goes on childcare, so I don't actually earn anything from directing."

Despite such difficulties, all three look on the positive side. "Some people are clearly trying to promote women directors," Marianne Elliott says. "I think a couple of times productions have come my way *because* I'm a woman." Milly Still recalls: "I did try becoming a full-time mother, but it only lasted a month, because I got twitchy. So I'm happy to accommodate the stress, and not feel hard done by."

Katie Mitchell believes motherhood has benefited her work: "It helps me to understand in a more profound and accurate way aspects of the behaviour of people in plays who have children," she says. She also sees hopeful signs for the future: "I teach young directors a lot, and around seventy to eighty per cent of the students are female. This sea-change has begun to impact on the business in the last three years."

A Shared Experience

Theatre-in-the-round is limited to just a few theatres in the UK. When the Old Vic was temporarily transformed into this shape in the autumn of 2008 for a production of The Norman Conquests, *I canvassed the views about this type of theatre from its leading exponents, including Sam Walters and Alan Ayckbourn.*

AFTER THIRTY-SEVEN YEARS RUNNING THE Orange Tree theatre, Sam Walters' enthusiasm for theatre-in-the-round remains undimmed. "It puts the emphasis on the text, on the actors, and on the audience," he says. "Once you move the actors into the middle of the auditorium and surround them with the audience, you've radically changed everyone's relationship with everyone else."

Although this egalitarian theatrical form, which puts the actors and audience "in the same room", has been established in the UK for well over half a century, it is only to be found in a handful of buildings. In addition to the Orange Tree in Richmond, there is the Royal Exchange in Manchester, the New Vic in Newcastle-under-Lyme, the

Bolton Octagon, the Cockpit in Marylebone in London, and the Stephen Joseph Theatre in Scarborough, where Alan Ayckbourn became artistic director in 1972.

Most of Ayckbourn's plays were written to be performed in the round. "I found it an extremely liberating medium to work in," he says. "You can employ a sort of fluency, and a lot of things fall naturally into place. In the round everything is visible, and every square foot of the playing space is viable. It's very much an actor-controlled medium. It's the sort of theatre I love."

Ayckbourn's mentor and great influence was the actor and director Stephen Joseph, who had seen this radical new type of theatre in action in the United States. In 1947 the dynamic producer Margo Jones – dubbed by her friend Tennessee Williams the "Texas Tornado" – had established the country's first professional theatre-in-the-round in Dallas, and the idea had spread. Returning full of missionary zeal, Joseph ran a theatre-in-the-round company in London, staging plays at the Mahatma Gandhi Hall in Fitzroy Square. Then in 1955 he established a tiny theatre-in-the-round in the public library in Scarborough.

At his death Ayckbourn took over as artistic director of the theatre, which moved into a school in 1976, and then to its present permanent home in a converted cinema in 1988. "Stephen's love of the round was based on the immediacy of it," Ayckbourn recalls. "His great concept – which I agree with – was that the only things that mattered about theatre, when it came to it, were the actors and the audience. Theatre-in-the-round, more than any other medium, emphasises this most strongly. The actors are in the middle, the audience surrounds them, and there's nothing else there."

As a radically different form of theatre it requires

particular skills on the part of the director, most obviously the need to keep the action flowing. It also puts a different kind of pressure on the actors. Chris Monks, who recently succeeded Ayckbourn as artistic director at Scarborough, has staged many productions at the New Vic, co-founded in 1962 by Stephen Joseph and Peter Cheeseman. "If actors don't have a hang-up about their relationship with the audience, they can find it incredibly freeing," he says. "They don't have to worry about being seen, or about standing in a particular place. But they still need to use their vocal technique for the benefit of people behind them, who at certain moments can't see their face."

Sam Walters believes you can stage virtually any play in the round, including Shakespeare. "His plays work a dream, because he didn't rely on grandiose sets, there's the actors' proximity to the audience for the soliloquies, and he tells you where you are." At the New Vic the community drama initiated by Peter Cheeseman, which explored historical subjects and local issues in documentary style, seemed especially well-suited to the form. "Those plays were important to the community," Chris Monks observes, "and being performed in the round they became a kind of debate."

According to Sam Walters, this kind of staging empowers the audience. "They need to be metaphorically on the edge of their seats thinking, Where am I supposed to be looking now? They can't say, Here I am, I've had a hard day at the office, I've sat down, now entertain me. It doesn't work as a form of theatre without a committed audience." He tells the story of the reaction of one Orange Tree regular, on hearing that the new theatre into which they were to move in 1991 would still be in the round. "Oh good," she said, "that means I'll still be trodden on by the actors."

Throwing out the Rulebook

In the spring of 2004 Tom Morris, artistic director of the Battersea Arts Centre, was made an associate director of the National. As he started his new job, he talked to me about the radical theatre groups around the country with which he hoped the National would collaborate.

THERE ARE MANY EXCITING NEW forms of theatre around the country, producing startling and high-quality work. As director, Nicholas Hytner wants the National to be actively engaged in bringing this kind of work into its programme. Part of my new job will be to do just that.

Until recently I was artistic director of the Battersea Arts Centre. The kind of work I was supporting there takes a very unusual route towards a final production. Often it starts with just a group of people with a few ideas. Sometimes there's a writer involved, sometimes there isn't; sometimes it's clear who the director is, sometimes it isn't. A lot of the work develops gradually through a series of public performances, staged long before it's finished.

Most of the work starts with a "scratch night", when between three and ten companies or writers each show ten minutes of the beginnings of an idea. The aim is to create a space in which they can discover, in dialogue with an audience, the most appropriate language of live perform- ance to tell the stories they want to tell. That was how *Jerry Springer – The Opera* evolved there.

It's through throwing out the rulebook that radical possibilities for new kinds of theatre are stumbled upon. There are creative cells all over the place. One that excites me is Shunt, the company which has hired a railway arch for three years. They spent nine months developing material for a particular show, did without a press night, and showed it every weekend for thirteen weeks, a truly radical experiment.

Another group is Kneehigh Theatre, which works in a small converted stable in Cornwall, and has the most extraordinary collaborative process. Then there's Faulty Optic, an innovative puppet-theatre company, which develops shows in a draughty old warehouse near Huddersfield. And Duckie, a gay carnival/cabaret from Vauxhall, who have a show where you order an act from the menu, and they come and perform it on your table. It's a great event, that's now been snapped up by the Barbican.

I'll be looking to connect the National with these kinds of approaches, working on a portfolio of between five and ten projects. The principle I've discussed with Nick Hytner is, Let's work with these people and see what emerges, and then decide what might happen. Some projects might be confined to the Studio; others, if they deliver well, might end up in the open air or the Cottesloe, or even in the Lyttelton or Olivier.

One challenge with these projects will be to decide how you integrate a writer into the process. Some writers don't like writing in isolation from the rehearsal room; they do it because that's how it's done, but they would love to be involved more fully. I look forward to brainstorming with Jack Bradley, the National's new-plays specialist, who is brilliant at working with writers. It's an area where we need to collaborate.

Breaking the Mould

In the spring of 2005 the National was pushing out the boundaries of music theatre, and encouraging young talent to spread their wings. I talked to Clive Paget, the theatre's music-theatre consultant, about its current projects and experiments, involving among other musicians Nitin Sawhney, Luke Haines, Rufus Wainwright and David Byrne.

FIVE PLAYWRIGHTS AND FIVE COMPOSERS recently spent an intensive week in the National's Studio, working in pairs on new ideas for music theatre. The results are already bearing fruit.

"We locked the door, threw away the key, and waited to see what they would come up with," says Clive Paget. "The results were very diverse, from a futuristic musical set in Cairo to a piece based on Philip Larkin's *The Whitsun Weddings*. We're already encouraging writer Justin Young and composer Nick Powell to develop their exciting, original idea for a musical set in London."

This bold, unusual experiment is typical of the National's determination to broaden its work, especially in music theatre. Since Nicholas Hytner took over as director nearly two years ago, much time and energy have been spent on encouraging partnerships between practitioners from different art-forms, and searching for talented young composers.

One unusual collaboration already in progress is *Trust*, a multi-media piece using music, video and dance. It's an exciting fusion between artists from different traditions that brings together world-music composer Nitin Sawhney and the contemporary kathak dance-maker Akram Khan. A recent two-week workshop on the draft script with actors, dancers and musicians brought about some radical changes, transforming a play with music into a piece of music theatre.

Another project is *Property*, a musical piece by

playwright Simon Bent and rock songwriter Luke Haines. It tells the story of the shady connections between the criminals of the 1960s and 1970s and the politicians of the Thatcherite 1980s. The pair were given a two-month attachment at the Studio, and the services of singers with whom they could test out their material. Subsequently a three-week writing workshop moved the piece on to the next stage. Although the National has decided not to stage it, it is helping the team to get it placed with another theatre or producer.

Today most music theatre comes from America, or else consists of a rehash of British pop music. For years the scene has been dominated by Andrew Lloyd Webber and one or two others, leaving little room for young composers and songwriters to have their work tested in a theatre. "Fifty years ago musicals used to be part of contemporary culture," Clive suggests. "Now they seem to be twenty years adrift. One way to change this is to encourage the talents of the younger generation, and allow them to work outside the normal commercial constraints imposed by the West End. We'd like them to think that you can write a musical about anything, rather than conform to the existing template."

He and others at the National, including associate director Tom Morris, are busy talking to a range of people who have no track record in music theatre, to see what creative opportunities they can be offered. The aim is to catch them early in their careers, rather than twenty years after they become famous. They include Neil Hannon from The Divine Comedy, Damian Gough (aka Badly Drawn Boy), the songwriter Rufus Wainwright, and David Byrne of Talking Heads fame. Many of the discussions are still at a very tentative stage.

The National is also supporting Next Generation, a

collaborative music scheme initiated through the Art of Regeneration project, in which young people will explore the connections between music, theatre, dance and the visual arts. "We want to develop people's ability to collaborate," says composer and workshop leader Simon Deacon. "We're not looking at product, we're exploring creativity."

Little work of this kind is being done elsewhere: with the adventurous Bridewell theatre now sadly closed, only isolated pockets of it exist, principally at the Battersea Arts Centre, the Stephen Joseph theatre in Scarborough, and Greenwich theatre. Hence the vital need for support for this new, risky and unconventional work. As Clive puts it: "If you can't break a few moulds at the National, where can you break them?"

The Identity is All

For the National's 1999 repertoire, Trevor Nunn and John Caird created an ensemble of actors to work together on six productions, including two Shakespeare plays, a Broadway musical, and works by Gorky, Bulwer-Lytton and Rita Dove. As the season ended, I listened to what the actors had to say about the experience.

THE RICH DIVERSITY OF THE six plays in the season was clearly a great attraction to Simon Russell Beale. "I went on my knees to Trevor to let me be involved," he recalls. "I love the idea of turning up and saying, 'What are we doing tonight?' And it's been a great joy playing all those different styles."

For the past year he and forty-seven other actors of differing ages, styles, ethnic backgrounds and skills have been in permanent residence at the National. It seems to have been a rewarding and generally happy experience. Despite the inevitable strain of a punishing schedule, and the demands of a complicated repertoire, the actors talk enthusiastically about the benefits and advantages of an ensemble set-up.

Gabrielle Jourdan says, "There isn't a better way to work." Raymond Coulthard believes, "You learn a huge amount working with such talented people for a long stretch." For Sara Powell, "The most important thing is the terrific support you get." Gilz Terera, who graduated from drama school only a year ago, says it's been a wonderful apprenticeship. "Everyone has been very helpful to me and very open. Because you're here for a year, you can learn something from one production and apply it immediately to the next."

One obvious plus has been the variety of parts on offer within a relatively short timespan. "Often you get typecast, but I've been lucky," says Simon Day. "I've had parts that really stretch me, from Ajax to various thugs and ponces." He and others speak of the respect the actors have developed for each other's work, the trust that has been built up more quickly than usual. As frequently happens – Simon Russell Beale cites the example of the RSC – the company spirit has become stronger as the year has progressed, to the obvious benefit of the later productions.

"By the time it got to Gorky's *Summerfolk* we knew each other very well," Raymond Coulthard observes. "Because you've been on stage with the others every night in previous productions, you develop a kind of shorthand." Gabrielle Jourdan agrees: "You felt at ease, you had that sixth sense about how people would react, which you wouldn't necessarily get with just one production."

Rita Dove's *The Darker Face of the Earth* is a play that relies particularly on teamwork. "By the time we got to it I trusted everyone," Sara Powell says. "We were part of an extended professional family, and I felt I could spout anything. It also meant you could sort out problems and disagreements much quicker."

The trickiest and most exhausting time for the actors was the early part of the year, when *Troilus and Cressida* and the musical *Candide* were in rehearsal simultaneously, with half of the company acting in both productions. As soon as these two plays were in performance, rehearsals began for Bulwer-Lytton's *Money* and *The Merchant of Venice*.

Gilz Terera remembers the pressures: "In the morning you were doing a battle scene in *Troilus and Cressida*, in the afternoon you rehearsed the 'auto-da-fé' in *Candide*, then you'd have to go back for a wig-fitting. It was a strain being pulled in different directions, but unavoidable." Actors with more than one leading role were particularly challenged, rehearsing one demanding part during the day and playing another in the evening.

Within the ensemble leading actors were able to accept supporting parts they would not normally consider, as happened with Simon Russell Beale in *Summerfolk*. "That's the true beauty of ensemble work," says Raymond Coulthard. "It adds an incredible richness to the production."

In the end, as with any company, so much depends on the chemistry between individuals, and their willingness to subordinate their personal ambitions to the needs of the group. The danger with an ensemble like this is that, if it doesn't work, the actors are stuck with each other for a year, and the lack of company spirit can infect six productions rather than one.

Happily, the consensus is that the ensemble has been a real success. As Simon Day puts it: "It has always felt like a team effort, even when people have felt knackered and dispirited. Morale has been terribly good, and everyone has worked incredibly hard."

11

Books on Theatre

Simon Callow – John Gielgud – Arthur Miller –
Edith Craig – Michael Blakemore – The National Theatre

Painful and Exhilarating

Being an Actor, *Simon Callow, Methuen*

"UNLESS YE BECOME AS THESE little ones, ye shall not enter the kingdom of art. It's neither comfortable nor easy to get hold of your child-self again, but it's behind all great acting and great theatre."

It's often said that actors are like children: inordinately self-absorbed, forever seeking attention or demanding approval. It's one of the many merits of Simon Callow's deeply satisfying and highly entertaining book that it forces you to think beyond such unhelpful generalisations.

Actors, he maintains, can make good use of their child-like qualities, since they are engaged in an activity that is "deeply and seriously childish". Creating a stage character is a form of rebirth: "You consciously unlearn all you have learned as an adult – how to walk, talk and think; you turn the clock back and start from scratch."

Being an Actor is full of wise saws about the actor's art – about the need, for example, for actors to locate a character in themselves, rather than rely on impersonation or mere understanding. Callow arrived at this position after a period in his career (during which he was labelled "Donald Wolfit on speed") when he subscribed to the glory theory of acting: "The actor as juggler, as magician, but also as weaver of spells and raiser of spirits; the actor as druid, dealing in images and archetypes; the actor as imitator, as stealer of faces."

What he had left out, he discovered, was the actor as *himself.* His book charts a journey of self-discovery: he uses his struggles with a variety of roles to highlight many of the most difficult technical and emotional problems facing an actor. As a result the book is infinitely more useful than the conventional acting handbook, because the ideas and convictions that Callow describes with humour and honesty have been dredged out of his own experiences, both painful and exhilarating.

The book is no less interesting for his attack on what he calls "the intellectual academic puritans", the university-trained directors who in recent years have taken over the prestige companies and subsidised theatres. Directors' concepts and company style have, he argues, reduced actors to little more than glorified galley-slaves. To prove his point, he describes some revealing modern instances of the Director as Dictator: John Dexter stalking Callow during the rehearsals of *As You Like It*, Bill Gaskill playing the martinet in contradiction to the stated democratic aims and structure of Joint Stock company.

Being an Actor is an unusual blend of autobiography, handbook and manifesto that reveals a great deal about the state of British theatre, as well as providing an excellent manual for anyone concerned about the purpose and process of acting.

All his World a Stage

Gielgud's Letters, *Edited by Richard Mangan, Weidenfeld & Nicolson*

AS IN THE THEATRE, SO in his letters: John Gielgud was a man of many parts, and acutely aware of his audience for all of them. In this comprehensive volume of eight hundred letters spanning nearly ninety years, we see him in a range of roles: star actor, generous friend, loving son, wicked gossip, indecisive director, anguished lover, brilliant anecdotist.

Some parts he plays with style, others with affectionate wit, yet others with sympathy, courage or blazing honesty. One of the many attractions of this absorbing and deliciously entertaining book is Gielgud's capacity for self-criticism. He was by his own admission vain, impulsive, often selfish, totally impractical in ordinary life, and quite oblivious to the world outside the theatre. "You know how blinkered I sail through life," he reminds one actress friend.

Yet it is precisely his obsession with the theatre that makes this book historically valuable. Gielgud stood centre stage in the English theatre for half a century, working as actor or director (and often both at once) in some of the finest and most influential productions of the day. His detailed, witty and sometimes despairing accounts of working with figures as diverse as Edith Evans, Noël Coward, Judith Anderson and Richard Burton provide a fascinating glimpse into the joys and woes of rehearsing.

I found much arresting new material here. Richard Mangan, a discreet but informative editor, has unearthed scores of valuable letters not previously available to biographers. They include many written to close friends – Irene Worth, Hugh Wheeler, Lillian Gish – that provide a wealth of new detail about Gielgud's work on stage and screen.

The letters to Laurence Olivier will prompt a reassessment of their complicated relationship. Gielgud admired many aspects of his talent, and often tells him so; yet there are also elements he dislikes. "His gift of mimicry (as opposed to creative acting) sticks in my gizzard at times," he tells one critic, while directing Olivier as Malvolio. To George Rylands he writes, perhaps not entirely in jest, "How dare you, sir, presume to compare my art with those two posturing mountebanks Messrs Wolfit and Olivier?" Yet Olivier, contrary to received wisdom, and despite his obvious jealousy of Gielgud, offered him several parts while he was running the National.

Among those Gielgud turned down were the Inquisitor in *Saint Joan*, Menenius in *Coriolanus* and Robespierre in *Danton's Death*. It's fascinating also to discover the many projects of his own that he failed to get off the ground, including a production of *The Browning Version* (a play Rattigan originally wrote for him, but he rejected), various attempts to play Brutus in *Julius Caesar*, Pirandello's *Henry IV* with Visconti as director and, on the film front, an Orson Welles treatment of *Death in Venice*.

The letters to his long-time lovers, Paul Anstee in England and George Pitcher in America, are the most personally revealing. As a gay man Gielgud was forced to live outside the law for most of his life. The letters show him to be an inveterate, often reckless cruiser. He continued to take huge risks even after his arrest for importuning in Chelsea – to which he reacts here with courage and dignity – and an attempted blackmail in New York, where he was rarely able to resist the gay bars and parties. His frank descriptions of casual encounters may shock what he used to call "my public". Yet these sometimes painfully intimate love letters also show him forging genuinely loving relationships, and attempting, not always successfully, to be honest within them.

As a writer Gielgud has style, panache, and an exquisite eye for detail. The letters are shot through with mischievous humour, and a delight in puns (*Lost Horizon*, set in Tibet, he retitled *Hello, Dalai!*). There are many unexpected, often waspish descriptions of theatre folk: Thornton Wilder is "a funny little nervous man, like a dentist turned professor"; Irene Worth in *Tiny Alice* "looks like a Blue Cross nurse who has lost her collecting-box"; Edward Albee is likened to "a surly pirate with a drooping moustache". But he often turns his wit upon himself. After his disastrous Othello he notes: "Quite a lot of people have come round after with tears in their eyes, but whether from boredom, horror, or pity for my temerity in attempting it, is rather difficult to judge."

Born into the theatrical Terry family, Gielgud has been often caricatured as an aloof, patrician, Edwardian figure, notorious for an ability to commit unintentionally wounding gaffes. This splendid book reveals an infinitely more complicated and attractive character: self-deprecating, down-to-earth and scurrilous, with an idiosyncratic gift for friendship, deep veins of loyalty and generosity, and an impressive desire to keep up with the times. We may not look upon his like again.

Surviving the Brickbats

Arthur Miller 1962-2005, *Christopher Bigsby, Weidenfeld & Nicolson*

FOR MUCH OF THE SECOND half of his life Arthur Miller was a man whose future lay behind him. The acclaimed American playwright, celebrated for classics such as *The Crucible, All My Sons, A View from the Bridge* and *Death of a Salesman*, struggled to get his later plays staged in his own country. When occasionally they were put on they were fiercely attacked by most critics, who thought them tedious, preachy and ill-written; as one typically said of *Incident at Vichy*, it was "the same old noisy virtue and moral flatulence". Miller, they decided, was a relic of the postwar era, stuck in the ideological struggles of the past, and totally out of touch with the modern theatre.

Yet while he was marginalised on Broadway, where moral seriousness was almost a sin, in Europe his plays were widely staged and enthusiastically received. This was especially the case in the UK, where audiences were clearly more ready to accept the theatre as a place where social and political issues could be explored. Directors and actors at the National, the RSC and the Young Vic readily embraced his work, both new and old.

These years were also marked by his unceasing activity in the public arena. Previously a persistent signer of petitions and letters of protest, he now became directly involved in political action. He was a major player in the anti-Vietnam War movement, and an outspoken and eloquent critic of the foreign policies of successive presidents, from Lyndon Johnson to George W. Bush. Perhaps his greatest achievement lay in his work for the writers' organisation International PEN. As its president for four years he campaigned tirelessly for justice for dissident writers suffering imprisonment under repressive regimes, in Russia, Czechoslovakia, China and elsewhere.

This second half of Christopher Bigsby's masterly and illuminating biography has all the virtues of the first. Rich in compelling detail, comprehensive in its coverage of his subject's private and public life, it tells Miller's tale with a fine narrative sweep and a sure grasp of the changing political background. While clearly sympathetic to his subject, Bigsby is not afraid to make criticisms, or to lay out clearly the arguments of Miller's detractors. He's an astute interpreter of the plays and of Miller's dramatic intentions, while his interviews with directors and actors involved in productions on both sides of the Atlantic provide valuable glimpses of Miller the craftsman in rehearsal.

The earlier book ended with the collapse of his celebrated marriage to Marilyn Monroe; the present volume focuses on his blissfully happy union of forty years with Inge Morath. A skilled and sensitive photographer with Magnum, a former lover of Henri Cartier-Bresson, she travelled all over the world, sometimes with Miller, sometimes alone. After Marilyn Monroe's excessive de-pendency, her independent character was clearly what Miller needed: she transformed his life, helping him at a critical time to regain his emotional balance and to resume his writing.

Given exclusive access to Miller's notebooks and his

unpublished works, Bigsby charts Miller's highs and lows in exceptional detail. It's a surprise to read that, by his own reckoning, he abandoned some ninety per cent of what he wrote. Despite his apparently confident public persona, he experienced many periods of depression, though not only as a result of the disdain poured on his plays. "There are times when you feel the whole weight of mankind on your shoulders," he once confessed.

Guilt about his past – notably his failure to fight in the Spanish Civil War or the Second World War, and his espousal of communism – was one motor for his plays. Surprisingly for a Jew, the Holocaust only gained his full attention after Inge Morath – whose father had been a Nazi – took him to Mauthausen concentration camp, and he attended the trial of several Auschwitz administrators and guards. After that, directly or indirectly, it often fed into his plays.

There are valuable testimonies from his daughter Rebecca and his sister Joan, both of them clear-eyed and eloquent in assessing his character, flaws and all. We see him at ease in his Connecticut home, planting trees and building furniture, or successfully intervening in the case of a local boy wrongfully accused of murder. Bigsby also deals sympathetically with the traumatic episode of the Down's syndrome baby, and the couple's much-criticised decision to place him in a home.

Despite the critical brickbats in America, Miller showed remarkable resilience and persistence, continuing to write into his eighties, believing his time would come again. He was right. Beginning in 1984 with a revival of *Death of a Salesman*, starring Dustin Hoffman as Willy Loman, Broadway began belatedly to make amends. Today, as Bigsby reminds us in this superb testament to a great playwright and a fascinating human being, "there is never a moment when an Arthur Miller play is not being staged somewhere in the world".

Forthright to a Fault

Edy Was a Lady, *Ann Rachlin, Matador*

HER MOTHER WAS ELLEN TERRY, the most admired actress of the day. Her brother was Edward Gordon Craig, the celebrated stage designer. Little wonder that Edith Craig was overshadowed for most of her life by two such towering figures.

Yet her theatrical achievements were substantial. She was a talented costume designer and maker, the founder of the radical theatre group the Pioneer Players, and an indefatigable producer and director of countless plays and pageants. She also played an important role in the suffrage movement, staging many feminist plays, and lived in a famous artistic lesbian *ménage a trois*. After Ellen Terry's death she turned her cottage Smallhythe Place in Kent into a permanent museum dedicated to her memory, and established the Barn Theatre in the garden, where leading West End actors such as her cousin John Gielgud, Peggy Ashcroft and Edith Evans took part in an annual summer performance.

It was her personality which held her back from achieving more. She was brusque, stubborn and invariably in the right. Nicknamed "Boney", her style of directing was dictatorial; Virginia Woolf satirised her as the bossy pageant organiser Miss La Trobe in her novel *Between the Acts*. When it was suggested she might join the Old Vic, Lilian Baylis remarked: "We don't want Edy here, she would upset the staff." She once threatened to fine actors who forgot their lines. Yet many of them admired her ability and perceptiveness as a director: Sybil Thorndike, who remembers coming away from rehearsals "bruised beyond words" after "a lashing", considered her a genius.

Her steeliness was present from early childhood. When her brother Teddy cried and said he was afraid of the dark, she exhorted him to "Be a *woman*!" Forthright to a fault, at the age of eleven she criticised Tennyson's new play to his face, after the poet had read it to her mother and Henry Irving. Later she ticked off Irving, advising him to speak as naturally on stage as he did off it.

Her relationship with Ellen Terry was a complex mixture of mutual love and a struggle for power, each of them policing the other's relationships with men. Ellen twice made Edy break off an engagement, while Edy resented her mother's third husband James Carew, and refused to meet them together. Yet Ellen apparently accepted her daughter's lesbian household, which she set up with the writer Christopher St John and the artist Clare Atwood (Vita Sackville-West disdainfully labelled the trio "The Trouts").

Edy Was a Lady contains her previously unpublished memoirs, scrupulously edited by Ann Rachlin. Written after Ellen Terry's death, they provide detailed backstage recollections of the famous Terry-Irving partnership at the Lyceum, where Edy played several small roles. Often accompanying Ellen on tour, she gives a vivid account of a journey across America, and of encounters with luminaries such as Sarah Bernhardt, Lillie Langtry, J. M. Barrie and Bernard Shaw.

These clear-eyed, unpretentious and affectionate memoirs belie her dragon image, and will feed the growing interest in this undervalued theatrical pioneer.

Handling Olivier

Stage Blood: Five Tempestuous Years in the Early Life of
the National Theatre, *Michael Blakemore, Faber & Faber*

MICHAEL BLAKEMORE'S SPELL AT THE National, a tale of one
man and two governors, began in hope, but ended in
despair. Hired by the theatre's first director, the ailing
Laurence Olivier, who identified him as his successor,
Blakemore directed a string of brilliant productions,
including *The National Health, Long Day's Journey into
Night* and *Front Page Story.*

But when Peter Hall took over as director he became
disenchanted with the way the theatre was being run. In
particular he believed the planning committee, of which he
and the other associate directors were members, was merely
a charade, and too often a rubber-stamp for decisions
already made by Hall. After a dramatic confrontation on
this issue he resigned, and never worked again at the
National while Hall was in charge.

Prompted by the publication of Hall's *Diaries*, which he
felt misrepresented those events, he here offers his version
of the unfolding backstage drama, as the National moved
from its temporary home at the Old Vic to its permanent
home on the South Bank. It's a balanced, cogently argued
account, in which he confesses to misjudgements and
occasional naivete, and is able to describe Hall as "an
impresario of genius" while criticising what he saw as his
hunger for power and money.

But his revealing memoir is not just about the
"strategies, alliances, secrets and betrayals" that marked his
tempestuous years at the National. It also provides
wonderfully illuminating insights into the way a director of
great flair, imagination and sensitivity handled star actors

in rehearsal, most notably Olivier himself in *Long Day's Journey into Night*, but also an alcohol-fuelled Anthony Hopkins, grappling unsuccessfully with Macbeth.

Once an actor himself, Blakemore handled the unpredictable Olivier with consummate skill, bringing forth a towering performance in Eugene O'Neill's masterpiece that revived the National's artistic reputation and its faltering finances. He sums up astutely the ambivalent feelings Olivier the administrator provoked among his colleagues: "He was not content with being *liked*; he wanted to be *loved*, and for the most part love is what we gave him; but it made for turbulent relationships, forever swinging between acquiescence and revolt."

The book contains a perceptive portrait of Ken Tynan, the influential critic who became the National's literary manager, and played a key role in helping Olivier to create an adventurous repertoire and a richly talented ensemble company. Written with passion and style, *Stage Blood* is a riveting inside story of a pivotal moment in the National's early history.

One Drama after Another

The National Theatre Story, *Daniel Rosenthal, Oberon Books*

IN 1976, AS THE NATIONAL THEATRE moved into its new home on London's South Bank, its literary manager Kenneth Tynan observed: "It's taken 128 years to get here: sixty of Victorian idealism, half a century of dithering, and a final thirteen years in the planning and building."

Today, under Nicholas Hytner's dynamic and broad-church directorship, the National is in rude health both artistically and economically. But as Daniel Rosenthal makes clear in this magnificently detailed history, published to mark the theatre's first half-century, the journey has been a supremely hazardous and contentious one.

Right from its Victorian beginnings, the idea of a state-subsided theatre was met with indifference, cynicism and hostility, not least from West End theatre managers and actors: Charles Wyndham called it "alien to the spirit of our nation", while Seymour Hicks wondered "if there are really half a dozen people insane enough to think it will ever come into existence". As late as 1961 John Osborne, fearing "some kind of awful museum", declared: "If it is ever built I only hope someone sets fire to it."

Yet the first detailed blueprint for the creation, organisation and management of such a theatre, provided in 1904 by Harley Granville Barker and William Archer, gradually gained support – though only after decades of committee wrangling, continual changes of site, and government reluctance to fund it. And when Denys Lasdun's brutalist concrete building finally rose up by the Thames, it attracted massive public opprobrium; in one poll it was voted the "Worst Building" in Britain.

Rosenthal, who spent ten years on the book, has had full and unfettered access to the National's extensive archive of letters, memos and board papers, and has interviewed a hundred actors, directors, playwrights and administrators. The result is a full and fascinating account of the contrasting regimes of the theatre's first five directors: Laurence Olivier, Peter Hall, Richard Eyre, Trevor Nunn and Nick Hytner.

Each had to confront similar challenges in the perennial battle between art and money: how to stage new, often experimental plays while balancing the books; whether to create an ensemble company or make use of the star system; how to attract new audiences beyond the traditional middle-class one; and how to keep the theatre open for business in the face of government cuts.

The stress was predictably enormous. Olivier saw the job as "the most tiresome, awkward, embarrassing, forever-compromise, never-right, thankless fucking post that anyone could be fool enough to take on". For Nunn it was like "juggling plates, while riding a unicycle, on a tightrope, over Niagara Falls", while Eyre suggested that "the combination of doing productions and attempting to be thoroughly on the case in every area is a one-way ticket to the madhouse."

At the Old Vic, the National's temporary home in the early years, Olivier created and headed a scintillating company, which included Maggie Smith, Michael Redgrave, Joan Plowright and Tom Courtenay, as well as emerging stars such as Derek Jacobi, Michael Gambon, Lynn Redgrave and Robert Stephens. But his tenure was beset with problems, not least his own debilitating illness, and his volatile relationship with Tynan, who favoured more challenging plays that reflected matters of public debate. Olivier also had to contend with censorship, at the hands both of the Lord Chamberlain and his own board; the latter was reflected in his battle to stage Rolf Hochhuth's controversial play *Soldiers*, with its potential libel of Winston Churchill.

His successor Peter Hall's great achievement was to oversee the transfer to the South Bank, and then just to keep the new building open: his battles with recalcitrant builders and striking trade unions would have crushed a less resilient and courageous man. He was undoubtedly a great impresario, a fine inspirer of talent, and a combative spokesman for the theatre in general. But his later years were overshadowed by his rash decision to take on other commitments at Glyndbourne and elsewhere, apparently putting his desire to make money before the needs of the National. Interestingly, he denies this charge today, telling Rosenthal: "I certainly knew if I was selling the National short, and I don't believe I was."

Like Hall, Richard Eyre had a passion for new writing, and was also responsible for bringing in black and Asian actors and giving greater opportunities to women directors. Yet, ironically, it was staging the musicals *Guys and Dolls* and *A Little Night Music* that enabled him to overcome the worst box-office slump in the National's history. As a leader he was clearly much loved and admired, but often felt insecure about his own abilities as a director.

By contrast, Trevor Nunn's undoubted brilliance as a director led to accusations that he "escaped" too often into the rehearsal room. This was to the obvious detriment of his managerial role, in which he proved frustratingly slow to make decisions. His policy of staging musicals was financially successful, but was lambasted by many critics for betraying the basic principles of the National.

Nick Hytner's reign, now nearing its close – Rufus Norris takes over in 2015 – has been remarkable for its audience-expanding cheap-ticket scheme, and for the opening up of the National to a greater range of innovating companies, such as Kneehigh and Improbable Theatre. A bold radical reformer, Hytner has also introduced Sunday opening and NT Live, which now brings the National's productions within the reach of cinemagoers worldwide.

Throughout the book Rosenthal describes with admirable lucidity and fairness the many dramas and crises, providing a variety of opinion and perspective from the main players, both now and at the time. Occasionally, as with Tony Kushner's *Angels in America* and David Hare's *Stuff Happens*, he gives rather too much space to plot detail. He also pays scant regard to the important and visionary work with schools and youth groups of Jenny Harris and her influential education department.

But these are only minor flaws in this meticulously researched book, which provides a uniquely revealing story of life within this great theatrical institution, which has provided so much pleasure, uplift and stimulation during its first half-century.